Academic lovers

Seline Mishon

Contents

01 | I'm better than you in every way possible

"It's not my fault that I'm just better than you in every way possible," he smirked as he leaned in close.

I take a step back, fighting the urge to smack him in the face. My features are clearly displaying my annoyance.

We're currently outside of second period, AP Lang, discussing the previous event that took place during class.

—

"Miss, it's obvious that Thompson doesn't have a solid fact to back up her argument," Aiden states with a slight smirk apparent on his face, his gaze fixed on me.I roll my eyes, avoiding his gaze. It's almost the end of class, and I still have one minute to back up my argument. The class is currently debating the topic of environments, and by the class, I mean Aiden and I."You have 30 more seconds left, Zhera; if you can't find a solid fact to back up your argument, then Mister Aiden's team wins." Miss Humingbird is giving me a pointed look.I nod, thinking hard and trying to find a way to win this. I could sense Aiden's cocky smirk from across the room. But I quickly shake my head, trying to stay focused.Since we've been placed in this class together, we always end up as opponents when it comes to debates. Neither of us is giving up. I know by now our classmates are used to this and just use us as a form of entertainment.I hear the bell ring, taking me out of my trance."Times up, Zhera; it looks like Aiden's team won today." Miss Humingbird boredly saysI sigh in frustration and start packing my bags, making my way out of class. I hear footsteps coming towards me and immediately frown."Hey sweetheart, it seems like I won again, not to anyone's surprise, though." He laughs, flashing that smile that I've seen so many times."Whatever Miller, this was a stupid debate anyway."He smiles for a moment, leaning on the wall."It's not my fault that I'm just better than you in every way possible, Thompson," he smirked, leaning closer to me. I hate it when he does that, obviously making fun of our height difference since he stands at 6 feet.I quickly take a step back, resisting the urge to punch him in the face. Annoyance is obviously showing on my features.I cross my arms over my chest, raising an eyebrow. "Don't get too cocky, Miller; I've beaten you way more times before."He smirks, turning around and raising one hand in the air. "Whatever you say, Thompson!"I roll my eyes and make my way to my locker.Aiden Miller is the embodiment of annoying and stuck-up. From his dark tousled hair, dark hazel eyes, and flashy smile, that's won all the girls. I've known him for the longest time and still can't stand him. We've been in rivalry for a long time, having most of our classes together, sadly. He just knows how to push my buttons.I sigh, making my way past the students in the busy hallway. I groan when I see people making out in the corner of the hall. This is Crestview Academy, one of the most prestigious high schools in the country, standing at the heart of the city. It's known for its amazing academics and fierce rivalries.In this school with smart students, some can be very dumb because they just make out in the hallways like this. Get a room.I roll my eyes before finally arriving at my locker. Suddenly, a face peaked out of nowhere. I jumped, but then signed after realizing it was Ciara."Ciara, how many times do I have to tell you to stop doing that?"Ciara shrugged. "Sorry, girl, it's just a force of habit."I rolled my eyes before shutting my locker and taking out my books for science, which is my least favourite class."So you know that guy that I've been telling you about?" she shyly says, changing the subject."Oh, yeah, the boy that you've been talking about twenty-four seven nonstop?"She blushed "Well, I've got some good news. He asked me out on a date."I gasped, squeezing her hand as we both started squealing in the hallway, earning a couple of glances. "Stop!, you have to tell me all about this, ok? Don't leave out any details; I'm serious."She chuckled. "Ok, ok, so-Before she could finish that sentence, the bell rang, and I groaned in frustration, putting my head back."Hate that fucking bell! I'll just tell you later, in class,"she says as we start making our way to science, which is also another class that I hate, like I said before, mainly because I have it with none other than Aiden Miller.

02 | Just the beginning

3 years ago

I sigh as I take a step out of the car, being cautious to hold my project in my hands."Zhera, you better win this; I didn't take a day off work for you to lose; you heard me?" My mother remarked firmly as she adjusted her blouse.I nod as she walks a few feet in front of me, and I begin to make my way to school quickly behind her. I know it sounds cheesy, but yeah, I'm currently in school on a Friday night for a science fair, the annual 9th grade science fair.Laugh all you want, but I enjoy science, and this is a big deal since the winner will receive a pretty good sum of money, maybe around one hundred.As we made our way through the door, I noticed a swarm of students and their parents frantically finishing up their projects.Taking a look at some of the students work and then mine, I feel a bit self-conscious. Will this even win?I decided to build a hydroponic garden, which took me days and several nights, but thanks to the heavens, I finished on time.Mom and I continued to make our way further into the school, heading to the gym where the fair took place, before someone interrupted us."Oh my goodness, Sadie? It's been a while, my dear!" A fruity voice exclaims from behind us.My mom stops in her tracks and says, "Hello, Madelyn, it's so nice to see you here!"Madelyn, who's that? probably one of Mom's work friends. She's very beautiful, though. Her hair is black and straight, while her checks are rosy and beautiful, painted with makeup.I awkwardly stand in the middle, pretending to be interested in the wall, as they talk for a few minutes about their jobs.A few moments pass. "And you must be Zhera, right?" The lady, who I suppose is Madelyn, turns to face me with a gentle smile.I grin sweetly and say, "Yes, I'm Zhera. Nice to meet you, miss."She shakes her head. "Oh, please, honey, no need for that; call me Madelyn. I used to change your diapers when you were younger; remember that?"I awkwardly smiled. How am I supposed to answer that? I was a freaking infant; of course, I wouldn't remember.I shake my head and say, "Uh no, sorry."My mom clears her throat, swaying from one leg to another. "So, Madelyn, what brings you here?""Oh, I'm just here to support my son; he's also participating in the fair. I was just with him a moment ago, but he decided to wander off somewhere." Knowing he still hasn't returned, she says that last line anxiously."Ahh, okay, we'll. My daughter, as you can see, is also competing in the fair."She turns her full attention to me. "Zhera, why don't you go ahead? I'll catch up to you later."I nodded, relieved to be free of that uncomfortable situation. My mother is no longer in view as I continue down the hallway, silently humming.I stopped in my tracks when I suddenly saw a figure coming my way.Wait, it's not coming, more like running.I squint my eyes in an effort to decipher who the hell is rushing towards me at top speed. As he runs, he bumps into a few people, not even apologizing. Why is that boy in such a hurry?As I continue to question, he gets closer and closer, and at the last second, I fail to get out of the way, causing him to collide into me and sending my project flying in the air.This moment feels like it's going in slow motion, like those scenes in movies."Noooooo!" I scream in slow motion as my project goes flying above our heads, trying to also shove the boy off me. His eyes also widen, his mouth hanging out in an O as he also watches my project fly through the air, dirt from it landing all over me.Vigorously cursing when the dirt ruins my favourite floral dressBack to reality when everything isn't in slow motion now. My project comes crashing to the floor; everything is destroyed."What the hell!" I cried, and as I scooted the boy off me, I sent him a glare.He's awkwardly scratching the back of his jet-black hair while giving me a nervous smile."Uhh, sorry," he shrugs as he starts making his way past me, not bothering to at least help me clean up the mess he caused.I grab his hand, stopping him from moving entirely past me. "You stop right there; I am not letting you off the hook after the stunt you just freaking pulled." I hissed, and he rolled his eyes."Well, it's not my fault that you didn't get out of the way like everyone else." The lunatic's tone is stern but slightly irritated.I tighten my grasp on his hand, stomping my feet in protest. "Listen here, you dim-witted lunatic; did you not think of not running through the halls like a maniac at full speed, especially during a science fair where there would be lots of people with their projects? huh?!" He flinched a bit but quickly regained his demeanour: "Look, I'm sorry for what happened, but this isn't entirely my fault, okay?, so I'm sorry. Are you happy now?"I sigh in disbelief. "Do you honestly think—" Before I could finish my sentence, he cut me off."Listen, whatever your name is.""It's Zhera.""Yeah, Zhera, I'm sorry, alright? Let's just call it a day and not let this ruin the fair."The hell does he mean not to let this ruin the fair; he literally decapitated my project and expects me to "call it a day?"As I stand there in disbelief, he stares at me with his hazel eyes, which are filled with nothing but boredom."Happy now? Bye."The boy, whose name I never caught, makes his way past me and heads to the gym. I'm still frozen in place, dumbfounded to even hear the announcer start the introductions."Hello, ladies and gentlemen, to the annual 9th grade fair!"—

Guess who that boy was? You guessed it? Yes, none other than Aiden freaking Miller.What an amazing encounter, right?Later on, I got to know his name by hearing the announcer yell it as the winner of the fair, with his mom, Madelyn, jumping in excitement beside him and Aiden flashing that famous smile of his to the crowd.To this day, that name still rubs me the wrong way.That night, my mom gave me an earful about how I'm so clumsy and that it would be the last time she ever took a day off of work to help me with something.To this day, she still stuck to her words. WonderfulThat was my first encounter with Aiden Miller, and I hoped that it would be the last, but little did I know that that was just the beginning.

—

Make sure to comment and vote! love y'all byeword count: 1194

03 | Kill me now

We make it to class in plenty of time before Miss Marsha arrives. Seeing that she's running a bit late, Ciara continues to tell me all about that boy she likes.

"Okay, so he's new to town, as you already know, and he wanted me to take him on a date so that I could show him around."

I squeezed her arm. "Aww, my baby is all grown up, going on dates with boys."

She giggles, somewhat flushed.

"Which is something that can never happen to you, Thompson."

I groan as I hear that aggravating voice, knowing exactly who it belongs to. "Stop projecting Miller." I turn to face him, and yes, he sits right behind me. It seems like the odds aren't in my favour. If that makes any sense,.

First, he is in nearly all of my classes, and to rub salt on the wound, we sit close to each other. Just great, huh?

"Sweetheart, you know that is completely wrong, right?" He smirks as he leans back on his chair, his hair falling a bit on his face.

I roll my eyes, turning around, knowing that he's right—Aiden has over half of the school's female population at his feet. Everyone knows that, and there is no denying it, sadly.

I am not attempting to start another argument. I let out an exaggerated sigh, turning my full attention back to Ciara and gesturing for her to continue.

She smiles and says, "Anyways."

Before she could finish her sentence, the same irritating voice called out once again.

"Sorry to interrupt, ladies, but Thompson, you know about the test, right? that teacher is giving out today?" He says this, leaning forward and giving me his full attention.

"Of course I do, Miller."

"Hm, well, I hope you didn't forget our little bet." He recalled it with a smile.

I roll my eyes. "Nope, not a chance. If I get a higher mark, you will have to buy me lunch for the rest of the month."

"And if I get a higher mark, which I will, you sit beside me for the rest of the month," Aiden added in an amused tone. I have no idea why he chose that for his part; that doesn't benefit him in any way. But then again, he'll probably use that opportunity to annoy the hell out of me.

I scoff, ignoring his cunning remark. "Well, let's see." I replied as Miss. Marsha finally arrives, with sheets of paper on her hands and sporting her signature pinched expression.

The class quiets down, and everyone gets into a stiff position. Knowing how she gets up in the morning.

She clears her throat, staking the papers on her desk and adjusting her blouse. "These papers I have here are your graded test sheets from last week; I'll start passing them down now."

I was stiff while adjusting myself to my seat. I suddenly hear a snicker behind me.

"Calm your nerves, Thompson, and start getting ready to be my seating partner." He says the last part in a humming tone, something he tends to do for some reason.

"We haven't even gotten our test yet; what makes you so sure?"

I get interrupted by Miss. Marsha placed my sheet on my desk, facing the back.

"I expected more from you, Zhera," was all she said.

I quickly took the test, feeling my heart sink. 95%—seriously, 95!— I internally groaned. Not ready to face Aiden's endless teasing. I mean, don't get me wrong, a 95 is not bad, but for me, it's not ideal; it is considered one of my lowest grades. So having it in science, which is my favourite and best subject, is gut-wrenching.

I'll have to talk about this with Miss. Marsha later

"Psst Zhera, what'd you get?" I hear Ciara's airy voice, and she shows me her sheet of paper, reading 65% in bold red with a thumbs up at the top right.

"I got a 65%; honestly, I'm not disappointed; it's my highest grade in this class, and plus, I got a thumbs up!" She shrugs while being proud of getting a thumbs up.

I give her a half-smile. "Proud of you, C."

"So what did your smartass get?" I carefully slide my paper towards her; she raises her eyebrows in surprise, not expecting this mark from me. "Woah, I don't think I ever saw that grade on your test sheets."

I groan, putting my head back in frustration, immediately regretting it. When I see a cocky smile on Aiden's face, he starts lifting his sheet, and I see a 99% in bold. Fuck

I quickly put my head back, groaning at the thought of him getting a much higher grade than me. I remember the bet he placed, which was that if he wins, I'll sit beside him for the rest of the month. There's 30 more days left in the month, by the way, so imagine how I feel right now.

"Thompson." I hear Aiden call out my name in a very amusing tone. I can just imagine a cocky expression lingering on his face.

"Miller," I firmly state, not turning around.

I then noticed Ciara in my rear view, who had a similar amused expression on her features.

Rolling my eyes, wanting to get this over with, I hurriedly placed my sheet on his desk, facing the back. I don't even bother to see his expression. I then slouch on my chair in embarrassment.unable to face him.

A few seconds pass, and I hear a whistle coming from behind me, followed by a "tsk,tsk,tsk." I groan, shutting my eyes, then hear movements from behind. A few seconds later, I'm surprised by the sight of Aiden crouching in front of my desk and placing his hands on it.

"I honestly didn't expect this from you, Thompson. Is everything okay? something you want to talk about?" He remarks sarcastically with a grin, sliding the paper back on my desk, facing down.

I briefly gaze into his hazel eyes for a few seconds, knowing what he's thinking: "Wow, she's stupid," "no way she got a 95," "ha! I'll never let her hear the end of this" or something like that. I huff, placing my hands around my chest and repositioning myself on my seat.

Aiden looks me in the eyes for a moment, then smiles, tilting his head a bit to the side. "It's alright, Thompson; I'll be the best partner you'll ever have," he states, emphasizing the word best.

"I'm not looking forward to it."

"Don't worry, I'll treat you wonderfully."

"Just go back to your seat, Miller."

"I quite like it here—the view, I mean."

"..."

"MR. MILLER, RETURN TO YOUR SEAT THIS INSTANT." The loud voice of Miss Marsha can be heard echoing across the classroom; best believe even the other classes down the hall heard her lion-like scream. I hold in my laughter, covering my mouth.

He doesn't give her a thought and just winks at me before heading back to his seat. Typical, he seems to not care much about school but still aces every test, which drives me crazy.

5 minutes later

Miss Marsha starts the lesson. I made the decision to pay close attention today since my grade wasn't ideal. I take very precise notes while blocking out all sounds other than Miss Marsha's voice.

"Here is a question to prep you guys for the next test." I quickly got out of my trance. Next test? I hear the whole class suddenly groan at that.

"But miss, we just had one last week! This isn't right.

The class starts complaining all at once.

"We have other classes, you know."

"This isn't fair."

"We're overworked"

Miss Marsha sighs, shaking her head."Do I look like I care about the test you had? That was in the past; we're now in the present. Plus, this test is to prep you all for the final exam." She clarifies, strictly raising an eyebrow.

Exam?, The school year just began, and she's preparing us for the exam that's in eight months. I sigh, scratching my head. Let's just get this over with.

The class eventually settles down, but I could still sense the tension in the air, which is totally understandable because what kind of teacher gives a test one week after another?

"Okay, now that you all stopped yelling like a bunch of zoo animals, I'll return to my original question: who can tell me which blood type is the rarest in humans?"

I instantly raised my hand, seeing that no one else did, except for Aiden. Miss Marsha deliberates before choosing.

'Zhera"

"AB," I answer confidently. Biology is both my favourite and strongest subject in science.

"Correct. Next, what are the two main divisions of the human nervous system?"

Once again, I quickly raised my hand.

"Aiden"

"Central nervous system and the periheral nervous system, also known as NS and PNS" Aiden answers in that confident voice. Oh yeah, I forgot to mention that biology is also Aiden's strong point.

The class sighs, knowing what's about to go down.

"Nice ! Next, this is a harder one. What are the three types of neurons?"Both Aiden and I raise our hands quickly.

She takes a while, glancing around the room. "Somebody else wants to answer?"

Crickets

Miss Marsha then sighs, also knowing what's about to happen, like it's a normal occurrence.

"Then I'll pick Zhera."

'Sensory, Interneurons, and Motor"

—

This goes on for a while, until the bell rings and everyone starts packing their things. Happy that Aiden and I's banter wasted most of the period.

"Wait, wait, wait! The bell doesn't dismiss you all; I do. Now sit back in your seats," Miss. Marsha sternly says it in a harsh tone.

Everyone quickly regains their spots, annoyed.

"I didn't realize time passed by so quickly; the brief quiz session took some time. Am I right?" She looks squarely at Aiden and me as she finishes the final sentence. OopsAiden shrugs, while I avoid eye contact.

"I was going to inform you all about the project you have."

"What, project?, but Miss, you never assigned us one." A random person blurted in a passive tone.

"Well, I'm doing it now; it's a group project consisting of only two people in one group, and I will be making the teams." Everyone groans at the mention of her choosing the teams.

I hope I'm paired with Ciara, but knowingMy luck, it'll be with somebody I don't want to be with. Wait, what if it's with... let me not finish that sentence.

"I have a sheet of paper here. It reads all of your names and your partners; I will say it out loud; make sure to listen carefully."

Miss Marsha starts naming the groups; some people were happy, some weren't. I was one of the unhappy ones since Ciara was partnered with someone else.

"And finally, Aiden and Zhera."

Oh, kill me now.

—

This chapter was way longer compared to the previous ones, I hope you all liked it!!

Word count: 1860

04 | Wrong number

"I'm home," I announce in a tired voice as I enter the house.

Silence

I shake my head since everything around me is completely silent. Like usual, it looks like they're not home yet. I drag my feet to the other side of the room.

Entering the kitchen, I notice a note on the counter: "Sorry, honey, your dad and I are working late today. Go find something for you to eat; don't forget to study too." —Mom

This is what I'm usually welcomed to when I come home from school: complete silence and emptiness throughout the entire house. Most days, my parents work very late, so it's just me at home.

I suddenly groaned as I recalled my teacher's announcement earlier in the day: she said that Aiden and I were a group together as a pair, and I was displeased—actually, I still am. I don't even know how to describe my current state of mind, but the only word I can think of is "pissed.".

After it happened, I urged her to change one of us, but she seemed uninterested in hearing me out, saying that her decision was final.

Aiden, however, merely remained in the back, snickering and finding the situation amusing. I am concerned that my grade may suffer because of how poorly Aiden and I get along when we're together. I am sure that Miss Marsha assigned us to each other out of spite. Doesn't she see how we interact together? God, please help me.

I purr my lips, shaking the thoughts out of my head. "Everything is going to be all right, Zhera." "Don't stress yourself over this." "It's just Aiden, nothing to worry about, I tell myself out loud as I pace around the kitchen, running my hands through my hair.

This is going to be the death of me.

You know what, Zhera, this is just Aiden; you're just going to have a project with him; you've known him for so long, so this isn't the end of the world. You can do this.

After I am done having that internal breakdown, I go to the fridge to see if there's anything to calm my hunger.

"Hmm, so we have cheese, chicken, and spaghetti; hmmm, oh, got it! I can make some cheesy chicken spaghetti, perfect."

Just as I was done taking out the ingredients, my phone started ringing. Who could it be at this time? Probably Ciara

I picked up the phone, questioning who it is, when I noticed that it's an unknown caller. I hesitate to respond, but I do, and I begin to wait for the other person to speak.

"Hello sweetheart" The smooth,deep voice of Aiden speaks, giving me a sharp pain in my head. I pause for a moment, debating whether I should respond or end the call.

"Stop thinking so much, Thompson; I know you heard me," he says, aware of what I was considering.

He seems to always know what I'm thinking, and it pisses me off.

"What is it, Miller? I'm quite busy right now."

"Oh, are you?" His tone made it clear to me that he didn't care.

"Yes, and how did you even get my number?" I ask, suddenly remembering that I've never given him my phone number.

"Your amazing friend gave it to me," he replied while chuckling, not bothering to tell me which one.

Ciara?

"Just get to the point; what is it?"

I hear rustling in the background. "Why in such a hurry, sweetheart? What if I told you I just wanted to hear your voice?"

"Miller!" I grunted.

"Thompson," he whispered calmly.

"I am this close to ending this call and blocking you," I threatened while putting my fingers close to each other.

"You're no fun, Thompson," he purred.

"Just not when I'm talking to you."

"You being fun? That is a highly unlikely scenario, so I highly doubt that, but I was planning to talk to you about the project."

A groan erupts from my throat, and I hunch my head back.

"Am I really that bad?" He asks in a pretend sad tone.

"Yes, yes, you are, anyway, as you were saying?"

"We should decide on a time and place for when we can start."

"But since we don't even know what the project is about, we should discuss it tomorrow. Miss Marsha promised to clarify tomorrow."I respond

"mhm"

A few seconds of silence passed. I was contemplating whether I should hang up now.

"So I also wanted to remind you of our little bet," Aiden said after the awkward pause.

Fuck. I totally forgot about that. Why did you have to lose Zhera by 95%? really. I even forgot to talk to Miss. Marsha is preoccupied with the whole Aiden situation.

"Oh noo, don't remind me about that too; it's as if you called me to ruin my evening."

He laughs, "Nope, just make it better.""Always ready for your new seating partner? I promise to be on my best behaviour."

"Shut up" was all I could say.

"See you tomorrow, sweetheart; don't be late."

The call then ended. I wanted to hang up first. I rub my eyebrows in frustration.

Oh, by the way, as part of the bet, I have to sit beside Aiden in every class that we share, which means four periods. I'm totally not ready for the long day that I'm going to have tomorrow.

The next morning

Ok, yesterday night I didn't sleep properly because, well, you already know why, so this morning I decided to go get myself a cup of coffee at the local coffee shop. I don't usually drink coffee; I'm more of a tea girl, but today I had to to keep me awake and give me energy for the long day.

After I got my coffee, I finally made it to school, trying so hard not to stumble on my feet.

What I'm glad about, though, is that I didn't have Aiden in my first period, making it my favorite. I also don't have any of my friends, which stinks, but at least I get to do my work quickly and relax since the teacher is pretty chill.

I yawned while taking my notes out of my locker, attempting to block out the noises coming from everywhere in the hallway. It's 7 in the morning, and these people are so loud. Each morning, I have to deal with this.

I slap my cheek and shake my head in an effort to feel more energized.

"Boo!"

I sigh, "Ciara, it's way too early for this."

She grinned while tugging at her black curls.Behind her ear and adjusting her uniform, she has chosen to wear the skirt today and paired it with some knee-high socks.

On the other hand, I decided to wear the pants since they're the first thing that popped out of the closet.

Ciara then scanned my face and said, "You look very tired. Is everything alright?" She asked in a worried tone while fixing my hair.

I simply nod.

"There! all better" She chirped after fixing the bird nest on my hair. She does this every morning. It's like our daily routine before class.

"Thanks; what would I do without you? I sigh while giving her a brief hug, nuzzling my face against the crook of her neck.

"No idea, Zehra."

We stay in a comfortable silence for a moment, then get interrupted when we hear a familiar voice.

"Hey bitches" The loud voice of Kehlani rang through the halls as she walked in our direction, earning a few glances from people.I chuckled while giving her a hug. "Are you going to do this every morning, Khe?"

"Of course, my parents finally surrounded me, so I'm going to make the most of this new-found freedom." She responded while hugging Ciara and flashing her bright smile at me.

Kehlani is one of my closest friends; this summer she was on house arrest for two months because, uh, she crashed her parent's car through her garage by accident, of course. I'll never forget that day. Ciara and I were witnesses. Her parents also decided to terminate her driving privileges, so every morning she either walks or takes the bus to school, which makes her late each morning.

"I missed you guys so much. Yesterday I missed the bus, so I decided to completely not come to school."

"Even though you could walk, the school is only five minutes away from your house, Khe," Ciara added, rolling her eyes.

"That's such a long walk, though," she complained while putting her head back. I just shook my head—typical Kehlani, the laziest person I've ever met.

"Anyways, enough of me. Tell me about that boy you've been obsessed with, C. What's his name again? Ryan? Mic-"

Ciara swiftly covers Khe's mouth. "Be quiet; don't say his name out loud." Khelani starts complaining, but her words are muffled against Ciara's hands.

"How about we give him a code name?" I suggest knowing that a code name would be way better than saying his name out loud.

She quickly takes her hands from Khe's mouth. "Did you lick me?" she asks, furrowing her brows, disgusted.

"Yes, teach you a lesson not to put your germ-infested hands on me," Khelani muttered while crossing her hands over her chest.

Ciara only rolls her eyes. "Ok, let's call him, uh, Pineapple."

"perfect"

"So he texted me this morning that he's going to be attending this school today and that I should meet him during lunch."

"Good luck, baby," Khe says as she squishes her cheeks, making Ciara giggle. I simply smile, happy for Ciara.

The bell suddenly rings, pouring rain on our parade. We say our goodbyes, then make our way to our classes, each going our separate ways.

—

Arriving to class, I make my way to my seat, being in the middle row at the corner close to the window.

The sky is currently clear, and the sun's rays create a stunning hew on the school grounds. It is the beginning of autumn, and the leaves are gradually changing colour, creating a beautiful scene outside. It is almost magical, with the birds singing, the wind gently blowing, and the leaves falling from the trees. Glancing at the entrance, I see some students cycling or walking, each engaged in a conversation with their friends, and some walking by themselves with headphones on. The scene is like a remake of the beginning of a romantic movie.

And I feel like the main character

"Zhera," I hear my name being called, quickly pulling me out of my trance. The whole class is seated in their seats, ready to start.

"Sorry, sir," I say while adjusting myself in my seat. Blushing a bit in embarrassment

"It's fine," Mr.Ray reassures, then turns his attention to the class. "Class, today we have a new student; come on in," Mr.Ray exclaims while gesturing for the person to enter.

The class starts whispering as the student steps in. It's a boy; he has short blonde hair and dark blue eyes, and his uniform fits nicely on him. He's pretty cute.

I hear some girls in front of the class whispering to each other.

"He's pretty cute."

"I know, right. I wonder where he came from."

"Do you think he'll say yes if I ask him to sit with me during lunch?"

"Aiden Miller is way cuter, guys."

Mr.Ray claps his hands together. "Quiet down, guys, and let him introduce himself." He then gestures to the boy to start speaking.

The boy clears his throat nervously. "Hi, I'm Michael. I came from another city, so I am new to the town. I hope we can all get along and be friends.

hm

"Thank you, Michael. Let's all give him a round of applause to welcome him to our class."

The class starts awkwardly clapping, and Michael just stands there, smiling embarrassedly. His eyes then landed on me. I quickly look away, going back to look out of the window. I groaned softly. I probably looked like an idiot.

" So Michael, you go take a seat beside Miss Zhera over there, the girl looking out of the window right now."

I quickly snap my head to the front, hearing my name. I always sit here alone, so I'm pretty annoyed that someone will be sitting beside me, but there's nothing I can do about it. I'll just hope he doesn't bother me.

He starts making his way towards my section, swiftly sitting in his chair. Giving me a quick glance with a hi. I simply smile at him, waving my hands.

Soon, the whole school will start talking about the new kid. He gained the name "the cute new kid."

Famous already

—

word count: 2143

05 | I win

"For the fifth time, Miller, I won't lend you my notes," I assert firmly while slamming my hands on my desk. Some of my classmates give me a confused glance.

"Thompson-"

I quickly cut him off by placing my hand in front of his face. "No; I said what I said."

Despite my assertiveness, Aiden gently takes hold of my hands, removing them from his face. He then gives me a "sad" expression before the corners of his mouth turn up in a playful smile.

Rolling my eyes at his antics, I snatch my hands out of his grip and say, "You really know how to push my buttons, Miller."

"Only you" was all he said in his playful voice while giving me a wink.

I furrowed my eyebrows in confusion and disgust.

We're currently in AP LANG, the first class that I have with Aiden, which is one of my least favourite classes, obviously. The start of the bet started today, as Aiden reminded me yesterday during that pointless call.

As the period started, Aiden wasted no time in annoying me. Despite the fact that it was a free period for us to prepare for our upcoming test, I struggled to focus due to the fact that I had this idiot beside me.

I start biting my pencil, something I usually do when I'm confused. I'm currently stuck on this question that I've been rereading for what seems like an eternity. English isn't my strongest suit. Even though it's the language that I speak on a regular basis, It's still not my best.

"B." Aiden leans close to me. I turn my head. Our faces are inches apart from each other. Catched off guard, I quickly avert my gaze back. "What?"

"It's B, Thompson," he repeats, his finger pointing resolutely at the letter B on the page.

I scoff "I don't need your help, Miller", knowing that I needed help.

"I noticed you being stuck on this for a while, Thompson," he sneered, rolling his eyes at my stubbornness.

"Ok, it wasn't that long, and plus, I knew the answers; I just needed to do my calculations." I huffed.

"We're in English, Thompson; what calculations could you possibly be doing?" He recounted that, while adjusting his sleeves and seeking the opportunity, I took the chance to scan his outfit.

He's currently wearing the uniform—a button-up long-sleeved shirt paired with a slightly loose tie.The uniform hugs his body nicely—I can give him that.

"Whatever, Miller," I say, dismissing him while turning my attention back to the sheets of papers plastered around on my desk. Taping my pen to my desk

After some thinking, the answer truly was B. Of course, he's right. Aiden has always been very good at English, while I, on the other hand, am not so good. Don't get me wrong, I'm good, but not that much compared to him.

15 minutes later

The class is totally quiet now, the only sound being the hum of the ceiling fans. Everyone was immersed in their thoughts and deep in their study sessions.

Even Aiden, which comes as a surprise to me, stopped bothering me a couple of minutes ago after I kept on brushing him off, not attempting to start our bickering, knowing that would result in me getting nothing done this whole period.

I glance in his direction, taking in his demeanour. He sat up right in his chair, jaw clenched, something I noticed he usually does when he's concentrated. His glasses were perched precariously on his nose; I also noticed him with them on sometimes. I'm pretty sure they're reading glasses. His intense focus was evident in the way he held his body still, his eyes fixed on the page before him. I can't believe I'm saying this, but Aiden looks kind of hot.

I quickly snapped out of my trance, abruptly averting my gaze, startled by my one word. Oh my gosh, eww, no way I said that. What the fuck?

I discreetly cleared my throat and redirected my attention back to my studies. Just ignore that, Zhera.

"Alright, class, to prepare for the test, we will be doing a quick debate or a mock trial. I will be dividing the class into four groups, consisting of 4 to 5 people, and assigning you opposing viewpoints on a topic. Each group can research and prepare arguments to present their case in a debate or mock trial format. You guys have to be quick; I'll give you 30 minutes to prepare."

Oh, another debate. my fav

5 minutes later

After a couple of minutes, the teacher finally finished assigning our teams. Aiden and my team will be going against each other. Which I'm happy about and eager to take revenge on the last debate we had.

I clap my hands, turning to face my teammates. "Okay, so first we should decide on who will be researching and who will be doing the majority of the talking. I'm okay with either; it depends on you guys."

"I can do the research." A shy girl with long black hair that cascades to her back says, I'm pretty sure her name is Aarna.

"Me too; I'm okay with that." A tall girl with ginger hair adds, raising her hand happily.

I nod "Okay, good. I guess it just leaves it up to you and me to do the talking." I say this, turning to my other teammate, who simply nods in agreement.

As we settle into our seats, we begin to prepare for the upcoming debate. The topic is whether genetically modified organisms should be embraced or rejected in modern agriculture. Which is a pretty tricky topic. We are against it, while Aiden's team is for it.

—

A couple of minutes pass, and I'm starting to practice my arguments; the debate is starting in a couple of minutes. I better be ready this time.

I shifted my gaze towards the other side of the classroom, which is where Aiden's team is situated. As I looked in his direction, I noticed something unexpected—hazel, piercing eyes staring back at me, and he was waving his hand with a smirk adorning his face.

With a subtle roll of my eyes, I silently mouth the words, "You're going to lose," to him. He shakes his head and mouths back confidently "We'll see about that, Thompson".

I scoff, turning my gaze back to my team, and I notice them staring at me.

"What is it?"

Aarna smiles softly, her voice filled with genuine curiosity. "We're curious as to why you and Aiden are always at each other's throats, like every day you're arguing about something."

Oh, hm, how can I explain why I hate that annoying, repulsive, vexatious, bird-brained fish?

I chuckle wryly, thinking of what to say: "He just gets on my nerves, you know, like he knows how to directly push my buttons, and I know he does it on purpose." That's the best way I could explain my dislike for him.

The other girl, whose name I now know is Salma, nods, looking up from her screen. "Everyone's been curious as to why you guys argue like every single day, haha, but it's entertaining."

I awkwardly nodded. Getting back to my work, I never really wondered how other people could persecute us or how our constant biking could be annoying, but whatever.

"Okay, let's go through what we're going to say. So you'll start with the opening sentence, while you two research what the other team's argument is about, and I'll try to counterattack their arguments. Got it?"

The three of them nod.

—

The class quiets down now; everyone is in their seats, ready to get this debate over with. Aiden and I's teams are going first. Both of our teams are in the middle of the class, facing each other. I could feel Aiden's stare, but I chose not to look up and distract myself.

As the debate begins, I take a deep breath. My teammate starts his opening sentence by explaining why we are against After my teammate is done, Aiden stands up confidently and starts his team's opening sentence by saying why they're for it. He made good points, and I can give him that.

As time continued, the debate became more heated, specifically between me and, yeah, you guessed it right, Aiden.

We've been going back and forth now.

"Your argument clearly makes no sense, Miller. I would like you to elaborate."

"Please explain to me where in my argument it doesn't make sense." He asks calmly while giving me a fixed look.

I clear my throat, looking at my notes. "You say here that..., but clearly that doesn't make any sense; could you please elaborate?" I say it calmly while tilting my head to the side.

"Mr. Miller, if you don't elaborate on your statement, your team loses." The teacher announces, raising her brows, clearly amused by our argument.

Aiden clears his throat, looking at his teammates for any help. They all shake their heads, defeated.

He bits his lips, then scratches his head. It looks like Aiden is at a loss for words, something that doesn't happen often.

"We would like to get a couple of seconds to talk this out." Aiden sighed while turning to his team.

"Make it quick," was all the teacher said while looking at her watch.

I pray that they didn't find a way to explain that argument; that made no sense.

A couple of seconds pass, and they stop talking. Aiden stands up, clears his throat, and looks me straight in the eyes. "We have come to a conclusion; we could not find any way to elaborate our statements."

I try hard to mask my smile. It looks like I won this one. I can't wait to rub it in his face.

—

How do you guys feel about their dynamic? Tell me your honest opinions :)

Word count: 1666

06 | Planning

"Miller" I cheerfully sing his name.

"Thompson" he deadpanned back, avoiding my gaze.

"How was the little activity we did?" I ask with a grin. A few minutes ago, we had a debate in Ap Leng, and guess who won: me! Aiden's team could not find a way to elaborate on their stupid argument, so that gave us the win. As soon as that class finished, I kept tormenting him about it, and now we're here.

He turns to face me, a pinched expression prominent on his face. A couple of seconds pass, and he smiles, that playful dimpled smile that I despise.

"It actually went pretty well, Thompson."

My grin quickly fades away. "You're so annoying" I reply, turning back around to face Miss. Marsha, who is setting up her desk,

"What? Thompson, You've been tormenting me about this for the past 10 minutes."

I furrowed my brow. "Duh, why wouldn't I? It's fun, to rub it on your face"

"Don't worry, I'll get you back"

"Uh huh, really? And how's that, Miller?"

He smirks, about to say something, before Miss Marsha clears her throat.

"If you two are done, I would like to begin my lesson."

I swiftly turn away from him and look straight ahead. I guess we got caught up. But Miss. Marsha appears to be at ease, as if she's used to this.

"So yesterday, I told you guys about your project and divided you into teams, right?" She asks, looking around the classroom through her glasses.

The class responds with a yes.

"Okay, so I will be explaining in detail what you will be doing, and for the rest of the class, you all can start planning on when and where you will start."

I place my head on my hands with a heavy sigh. Feeling a sense of frustration. This is what I was dreading. The fucking project had been paired with the person I least preferred to work on it with.

In my rear view, I see Aiden smiling while tilting his head to the side. I couldn't help but scoff inwardly: What's he so jolly about?

Miss.Marsha starts walking around the class while explaining the project. We will all have to do different work that centers around the same subject. She started explaining what each group would be doing.

"Finally, Aiden and Zhera, you two will be doing The Effects of Light Pollution on Nocturnal Animal Behavior." She stops at our desk, handing us a sheet of paper.

"This project would require a significant amount of research. You would need to consult scientific articles, government reports, and other reliable sources. So you must spend a lot of time together researching your topic. I would like to expect an excellent job from my two-star students."

Aiden and I exchange a quick glance and nod. Great, we have have twice as much pressure since Miss. Marsha has high expectations for us to deliver an "excellent job"

I take a look at the paper; it has all the instructions. It looks like the project is due at the end of next month. And of course, it counts for 35% of our overall grade. Great, we have a project at the beginning of the year that counts for 35% of our grade. This teacher can not be real.

"You should all look through your papers and start planning how you will start. Get to work!"She instructs the class. In a firm tone.

The class quickly becomes loud as everyone starts going to their teams.

I glance at Ciara, who is all the way on the other side of the class. She looks at me, pouting her lips, and then points at her partner, Matt. It seems that she's paired with someone that nobody likes—literally no one. Matt is considered weird and annoying by the rest of the class, and to make matters worse, he has a huge crush on Ciara. So I guess he's very happy about being her partner. I chuckle and wish her good luck.

I suddenly feel a gentle yet deliberate force turning my chair smoothly towards them. Startled, I blinked twice in surprise, only to find myself face-to-face with Aiden.

"Now that I've got your attention, let's start" he simply says.

"That was unbelievably unnecessary, Miller"," I muttered, crossing my arms in a defensive gesture.

A smile played on his lips as he responded, "It got your attention, didn't it?" His hazel eyes locked onto mine, challenging me to look away.

I averted my eyes and let out a sigh. "Whatever, let's just get started"

"That's what I thought; now let's plan when we can start."

I nodded. Taking a moment to consider my schedule, I continued, "So tomorrow I can't; since it's Saturday, I also can't on Sunday; I have a student council meeting; then that leaves next week on Monday"

"You're still in that student council thing?" He asks surprisedly, leaning out of his chair and getting closer to me.

I back away a bit, "Yeah, I'm president."

"Congrats"

I give him an expressionless look, "I got elected last year, Miller" something he was aware of.

"I know, I know, he chuckled. I was just playing with you; you do know I voted for you, right?"

My eyes widen in surprise.

"Really?" I exclaimed. During election season, Aiden wasn't really present; for some reason, he rarely showed up to class, so I never knew who he voted for.

"Why does that come as a surprise?" he questioned.

" I mean, I never expected you to vote for me, and plus, you were barely at school during that time."

Aiden scratches his head, clearly startled by my observation.

He quickly goes back to our old subject: "I'm also free next week on Monday; let's meet at the school's library."

"sounds good to me."

We stay in silence for a bit until the bell rings.

—

I wait for Ciara to finish packing her things, then we start making our way to lunch, the only time that the three of us—Ciara, Khelani, and I—can spend time together in school.

During lunch, Ciara talks about, Matt, describing him as the epitome of awfulness. Meanwhile, Khelani chimes in with tales of her 10th crush of the week.

As the day progresses, before I know it, I find myself arriving home. I glanced under the door step. The lights are on; it looks like they're home today.

Eagerly, I open the door "I'm home."

"Hello, honey" My dad greets me from his desk in his stern voice while typing something away on his computer. Not bothering to look at me

"Hi, daddy" I smile while giving him a hug. In return, he merely tapped my hands.

"How's school? Staying on top of your classes"Here comes that question: how many times are they going to ask me that question? It seemed like every time my parents asked, it never ceased to be a topic of conversation.

As I place my bag on the couch, my dad looks up from his laptop, awaiting my answer. "Yes, dad" I reply. "Oh, today, Miss. Marsha the science teacher handed us a project, and guess who I'm with?"

"Who?" He asks then returns his focus to his screen.

"Aiden flipping Miller" I reply, watching as my father's expression changes from mild interest to one of recognition. He glances away from his computer for a second, trying to remember where he heard that name before.

"Oh, that boy, how's he doing? It's been a while since I saw him."

I chuckle and roll my eyes. "He's as annoying as ever, don't worry." I use air quotes to emphasize my point.

"Zhera, that's no way to talk about your classmate." My father smiles , recognizing the familiar dynamic between Aiden and me.

"Well, I'm sure you two will make great partners for the project" he says, turning back to his laptop. "Just try to keep the peace and work together, okay?"

I nod in agreement, taking dad's advice into consideration.

Mentally preparing myself for the start of our project next week.

—

It's getting better, huh? Haha, I'm excited.

Word count: 1365

07 | night

"That makes your body look amazing" Khelani purred.

"It does, doesn't it?" Ciara responds with a confident smile, admiring her dress in her square-length mirror.

"I feel like you should lose the dress, though" I hinted while laying on the pile of clothes scattered on her bed.

Kehlani looks at me with a perplexed expression and asks "Why?"

I adjust myself on the bed. "Well, since both of them are going to mostly be walking around and do fun stuff, Ciara should wear something more comfortable but also cute."

Ciara continued to admire her dress while nodding in agreement. "You're right; I'll save this dress for another time."

We've been at Ciara's house trying to plan an outfit for her date with Michael for the past hour now. I was pretty surprised when I found out that he was the new kid in school, but obviously that would make sense. I don't know how it took me so long to connect the dots.

First Ciara talks about how he's new to town, then a new boy comes to school saying that he's new to town, and plus, the guy Ciara likes name's starts with a M is named Michael. How could my dumbass not know?

"So let's pick something that's casual but cute" Kehlani nods while making her way towards Ciara's enormous walk-in closet. Ciara has a love for fashion and collects any clothing she finds at the mall, which explains her huge walk-in closet stocked with countless tops, dresses, shoes, skirts, accessories, and way more.

"Ciara, with you having such a huge closet, a walk-in one at that, why are we struggling to find something good?"

She came to sit beside her after she changed out of the dress, shrugging her shoulders. "I have no idea; I guess planning an outfit is the hardest part." She looks at the time"Shit, it's almost 5 and I'm still not ready."

"Lucky for you, I found something; it's perfect." Kehlani exclaimed from inside the closet, her voice slightly muffled. With a beaming smile, she emerged, clutching a set of clothes in her hands.

It's a white, form-fitting tube top, complemented by a long-sleeved, fluffy beige cardigan and a pair of blue jeans.

"Oh my gosh, that's so cute; I don't even remember having these" Ciara exclaims in a cheerful tone.

Khelani and I shared a laugh at her excitement before urging her to try on the outfit.

She runs towards her closet, trying it on.

Khelani makes her way towards her vanity dresser, admiring the vanity and the well-organized things.

"Aww, she still has this" she says while pointing at a bracelet. I make my way towards her, taking the object in my hand.

It's the bracelet we made for her back in 8th grade when Ciara was leaving for the summer and we thought she would never come back.

I can still vividly remember that day.

4 years ago

" Don't forget me, guys" Ciara whispers in a croaky, raspy voice as she delicately pushes her short curls behind her ears. Her words hung in the air.

"Of course we won't" I managed to utter, my lips trembling from the weight of the moment, my checks flushed.

"You mean the world to us" Kehlani replies, standing beside me leaning from one leg to another, her eyes glistening with unshed tears.

She reached out and gently squeezed Ciara's shoulder.

Tears started streaming down my face uncontrollably, and I hastily tried to wipe them away, but they kept on cascading down like a waterfall, betraying my attempts to remain composed.

"Zhera, you're such an ugly crier" Khelani says in a croaky voice, a small smile tugging at the corners of her lips. I couldn't help but let out a weak chuckle amidst the tears.

"Shut up, Khe; this is supposed to be a sad moment" Ciara replies with a small smile playing on her lips.

She then sighs, "I'll miss hanging out every day after school and trying on all the clothes we saw at the mall."

"I'll also miss re-watching all the seasons of TWD and never getting bored." I add that remembering those moments, The Walking Dead was our all-time favourite show, and I lost count of how many times we re-watched it.

"I'll miss going to your pool at night and gossiping the whole time" Khelani chimes in with a soft sigh.

Chara and I both nod.

"The only thing I won't miss is Kehlani talking about her 5th crush of the day and how he looked at her, so that meant he wanted her"

We burst into laughter at that.

After we're done reminiscing about the memories, a serene silence settles between us. It was a comfortable silence, one that spoke volume without words. In that movement, time seemed to sit still.

However, our moment got cut short when Ciara's parents arrived, gesturing to her that it was time to go. The realization struck all three of us. We clung to each other in a tight hug that lasted for what felt like an eternity.

Minutes passed by, and we discovered that there had been a miscommunication on Ciara's part. She was actually meant to go to her grandma's house, which was just a 40-minute drive away from her own home. The confusion arose when she eavesdropped on her parents talking in the kitchen about "going away".

And so, the three of us stood there dumbfounded, our cheeks flushed with embarrassment and our eyes swollen from the tears that had threatened to spill over. It was a moment of both relief and slight embarrassment.

End of flashback

"Ciara really made us cry for no reason; she's so stupid sometimes." I sigh, shaking my head, remembering how, because of Ciara, our faces were puffy for the rest of the day.

The centre piece of the bracelet featured our initials, while colourful beads adorned its surroundings. Each bead represented our favourite colour: blue, pink, and purple.

"Now that I look at it, it looks so bad; this was definitely your fault, Zhera." Khelani is furrowing her brows.

I playfully shove her in response, knowing that arts and crafts aren't really my thing.

"I'm done" Ciara sings as she emerges from her closet, posing like a super-model strutting down a runway.

The outfit looked good on her; it was simple but cute; the tube top hugged her body nicely; and she paired it with cute gold jewelry that a adds a touch of elegance.

"You look so cute!" Kehlani and I both squealed in unison while jumping around Ciara.

"You look so good, I just want to eat you." Khelani says she looks her up and down with a smirk.

Ciara rolls her eyes with a smile while admiring herself in the mirror.

Suddenly, the sound of a car horn broke through the room, causing her to jump in surprise. "Looks like he's here, guys; wish me good luck!" she exclaimed, a hint of nervousness in her voice.

I gently rubbed Ciara's shoulders, trying to calm her nerves. "You don't need luck, Ciara" I reassured her. "Just be yourself, and everything will be fine" She leaned on me, letting out a sigh of relief. "Yeah, you're right" she agreed.

"Just be yourself" Kehlani advised, her voice filled with confidence. "If he doesn't appreciate you for who you are, then that's his loss. You deserve someone who loves and accepts you completely. Never get worked up over a man."

Kehlani was always good with her advice and had a way of making the situation feel less tense.

Ciara nodded her head in agreement; I could tell that talk made her nervousness leave.

A couple of seconds later, after she checked herself, she made it out the door.

We waved her off while seeing her walk towards his car, a white BMW.

I kind of found it a bit rude that he didn't come to the door to walk with her, but whatever.

Later that evening

As the sun sets and darkness envelops the surroundings, the pool becomes illuminated by artificial lights strategically placed around the area. The soft glow of these lights casts mesmerizing reflections on the water's surface, creating an ethereal ambiance. The cool night air embraces my skin.

The only sounds I hear are those produced by nature itself: the gentle rustling of leaves and the distant chirping of crickets.

I sighed, taking my head back and relaxing in the pool.

Kehlani is sitting behind me on the chair. We're currently at Ciara's pool while she's still on her date; we decided to take a late-night swim, plus Ciara has the best pool out of the three of us.

Taking a swim at night is by far better than one during the day. The darkness of the night adds a sense of tranquilly to the water, creating a serene atmosphere that is way different from swimming during the day.

Almost every weekend, the three of us take a swim in the pool; it helps us relax after the busy school week we had.

"So" Khelani breaks the silence. While adjusting her bikini, she's wearing a cute floral bikini top paired with a matching floral bikini mini short.

"How are you and Aiden?"

I quickly snapped my head towards her at the sound of his name. "The way you asked that question as if the both of us were together, never again" I replied, slightly annoyed.

Kehlani couldn't help but tease, "You guys might as well be together with the amount of time you spend together."

Rolling my eyes, I retorted, "Oh, please, the only time we're together is at school. We're forced to be close because most of our classes are together. And you know how I feel about him. Khe"

Kehlani has always shipped me and Aiden together for as long as I can remember. It's honestly so annoying, as she knows how I feel about him.

"Zhera, he's a catch, and you know that; he has dark hair and beautiful eyes, plus he plays football, and that body.. don't forget he's very smart too! I mean, he's the whole package."

She is right; Aiden is very good-looking. I can give him that. But that still doesn't excuse my dislike for him.

"Please, Khe, he just has a way of pushing my buttons, and I can't stand him. So enough with the shipping."

She simply shakes her head, giving me a "whatever you say" look.

The moon glistened on the water. The conversation with Kehlani had momentarily distracted me from the moment of relaxation I had. But now, as I lay back and closed my eyes, I let the warmth of the water wash over me.

A couple of minutes passed when I opened my eyes and glanced over at Kehlani, who was engrossed in her own thoughts. She had always been a hopeless romantic, believing in fairy tales and happy endings.

As much as I tried to brush off Kehlani's comments, they lingered in my mind. Aiden and I did spend a lot of time together due to our shared classes. But there was something about him that irked me.

Perhaps it was simply because he seemed to enjoy getting under my skin.

Despite that, I would focus on myself and my studies. And if that meant enduring Kehlani's constant teasing and shipper tendencies, then so be it.

—

I love these three's friendship so much!

Word count: 1922

08 | Awful day

I collapse onto my bed, exhausted from the long day. Today was the student council meeting, where we discussed ways to improve our school and also started preparations for the upcoming homecoming in the fall.

As the president, I bear the weight of staying on top of everything and organizing most of the events. On top of that, I have to ensure that my grades stay high. It's no wonder I'm feeling so exhausted.

Determined to make the most of the rest of my day, I decide to be productive and head for a shower. As I stand under the warm water, I let it wash away the stress that I had throughout the day. I take my time washing my hair, massaging my scalp with shampoo, and allowing the soothing sensation to relax my mind.

This is when I truly deal with peace—no teachers, parents, school, stress, and most importantly, Aiden.

After finishing my shower, I wrap myself in a fluffy towel and make my way back to my room. After I'm done getting dressed, I sit at my desk, damp hair dripping onto the surface. I open my backpack and take out my homework.

Just as I start to immerse myself in my work, I hear my mom's voice calling me from downstairs.

Sighing softly, I realize it's time to take a break. "Alright!" I yell back, trying to put some enthusiasm into my response. Slowly, I gather my things and head downstairs.

The house is currently quiet. The only sound being heard is from the kitchen, where my mom is. It looks like dinner's ready.

"Yes?"

"Set the table." She states that her attention is focused on the simmering meal on the stove.

I frown. This is what she called me here for?

My mother shot me a sharp glance, and I quickly got to the task. With my height of 5'7, I swiftly reached for two plates from the high shelf and placed them on the table.

"Is dad coming?" I inquired, although I already knew the answer.

"No, your father will be working late tonight," my mom replied.

I sighed inwardly, realizing that my question was pointless, as I was well aware of my dad's usual routine.

A few minutes later, mom and I are at the dining table, surrounded by an atmosphere of quietude. The only audible sound is the gentle clattering of the plates as we begin eating.

This was the typical routine with my mom.

Suddenly, breaking the silence, she clears her throat. "So, Zhera, how is school treating you? Are you managing to keep up with your studies?"

I look up from my plate, momentarily pausing to register her question. "Just the typical boring classes, and yeah, I'm studying."

She nods approvingly. "Good, I expect nothing less than an A."

I nod before returning my attention to the food in front of me, but I can't help but feel a sense of frustration. A day will never pass without her asking me about school. Every day it seems like the conversation revolves around school, school, and more school. When will it ever be about anything else?

I shake my head, getting those thoughts out of my head.

No, mom's right, school is important. I get what she's trying to say: I should keep up with my studies and get good grades; that will make her proud.

It'll make everyone proud. So I continue to smile and nod as she continues talking about school, pretending that everything is fine even though it's not.

The next morning

I slammed my locker shut after taking out my books. The weight of the morning had already taken its toll on me.

"Damn, Z, having a tough morning?" Kehlani remarked with a sympathetic smile, as she's skillfully pealing an orange with her bare hands.

I could only manage to wearily nod in response."Yes, stepping foot into this school has already ruined my morning."

With a gentle chuckle, Khelani extended a slice of orange towards me. "Want some?"

I shake my head, not being in the mood to eat."I appreciate it,but all I really need is a hug," I confessed softly.

Kehlani smiles and then warps her hands around me in a bear hug. Squeezing me tightly. "Alright, Kay, thanks, but you're suffocating me." I breathe out, motioning for her to let go.

She smiles, but it quickly wipes off as her gaze shifts behind me.

"Don't look," she whispers urgently, "but hotties, behind you, five o'clock."

She says, widening her eyes. I steel a quick glance over my shoulders and roll my eyes in response.

And there he is, Aiden, strutting confidently through the halls in my direction. His smug smile remains plastered on his face, and his black hair is slightly tousled yet still impeccably styled. It comes as no surprise that he looks like that even at seven o'clock in the morning.

Walking alongside Aiden is his friend Alejandro, whom I have occasionally seen hanging around him before. Alejandro has a certain charm with his long brown hair and pretty green eyes. He is considered a catch around here.

I frown as our eyes meet. With a mischievous smirk playing on his lips, he raises his hand in a casual wave before breaking into a jog towards me.

I turn around, rubbing my face, getting ready for whatever is about to come.

"hi"

His husky voice gestures towards Kehlani; she feigns ignorance, pretending not to see him, then looks up, surprised.

"oh, hi! , orange?" She croaks, handing him the one slice of orange she has left.

A faint smile graced his lips, shaking his head. No

He then shifted his focus to me. "Morning, sweetheart"

Letting out a groan in frustration, "Not right now, Miller," I grunted.

"What, I can't say good morning now?"

I raised my gaze to meet his, a hint of annoyance evident in my expression. "Well, it was a good morning before you arrived," I retorted sharply.

His head tilted to the side as he rolled his eyes playfully. "Always in a bad mood, huh?" he remarked teasingly.

Of course I'm in a bad mood; how could I not be in a bad mood when you're around me almost 24/7? It's like a talking bird following your every move.

"Why are you here, Aiden?" I say, gesturing for him to get to his point.

Aiden approaches me with a mischievous glint in his eye and a sly smile on his face.

"Come here," he says, quietly.

"No." I firmly respond, crossing my arms defensively around my chest.

He shakes his head. "Don't forget today after school," he leans in, whispering in my ear. Aiden's voice was just loud enough for those around us to overhear.

I lightly gasped.

He straightens back up, grinning widely, clearly pleased with himself. Then he proceeds to smoothly make his way past me.

I glanced over at Kehlani, who wore a perplexed expression on her face while smirking.

I roll my eyes, "Don't start."

Raising her hands beside her head and shrugging her shoulders, Kehlani replied innocently, "I didn't say anything."

I could tell she was dying to ask me what was going on after school with Aiden.

I let out a sigh, explaining, "It's just for a project. We're meeting up at the library.

She slowly nods.

—

It's last period now, which means a couple of minutes before Aiden and I have to meet up at the library

I find myself anxiously glancing at the clock while absentmindedly tapping my pen on the desk. It's 2:20; class ends at 3:00. Fuck, only a few precious minutes left

Frustration begins to well up within me as I realize that time is going way to fast. I shake my head and redirect my attention to my sheet of paper.

Last period is the fastest period for me, which I usually love, but today I hate it. I steal a quick glance at the wall, and guess what time it is already 2:35. This is not normal.

It's almost as if the Gods themselves are toying with me, they know that Aiden and I have this thing after school, so to torture me they have chosen to manipulate time to pass even faster than usual. That can only be the explanation for whatever is going on.

"Alright, class, hand me your papers." My teacher's voice broke through my thoughts. Shit, we were supposed to finish this small quiz, and I've barely done anything. I spent the whole period procrastinating about the Aiden thing

Fortunately, this quiz doesn't count towards my final grade. Reluctantly, I rose up from my seat to hand in my paper.

Glancing at the clock, I saw that it was already 2:40. Time seemed to slip away even faster as a few minutes passed.

And when I looked again, it was 2:49. My fingers start to grow clammy with sweat.

My restlessness escalated as my legs began to bounce up and down uncontrollably. Each passing second felt like an eternity. Finally,it was 3:00. Oh God.

The sound of the bell echoed throughout the classroom, signalling the end of class. Students swiftly gathered their things and made their way towards the door, eager to escape the confines of the classroom.

A mixture of relief and apprehension filled the air as we dispersed into the bustling hallway.

—

"Wish me good luck, guys," I muttered under my breath, facing Ciara and Kehlani beside my locker.

Ciara glanced at me with a smile, shaking her head gently. "Calm down, Zhera," she said reassuringly.

Her words were meant to soothe my nerves, but I couldn't help but feel a sense of dread creeping up inside me. This wasn't just any project; it was one that I would have to do alone with Aiden for an entire month. The thought of working closely with him for such an extended period seemed like a nightmare in itself.

I took a deep breath, trying to gather my thoughts and compose myself. "Yeah, it's just a project." Khelani chimed in while snacking on an apple. Where does she find all these fruits?

I pursed my lips in determination, nodding in agreement. "Yeah, you're right, guys. I just have to suck it up and get it over with," I replied, my voice steady.

"Good girl, now go." Ciara said, urging me to go to the library.

"Here, take this apple. It'll make you feel better," Khelani said, forcefully placing a slice in my mouth. I swallowed it, giving her a glare.

She just blew me a kiss.

—

"Miller"

"Thompson"

"What's this?"

"You tell me"

I groaned out loud. We're currently standing in front of the huge library door. And guess what? It's closed.

The sign on the door read, Temporarily closed due to malfunctions, sorry.

For God's sake, Can't this day get any worse? Of course, the one day we have to start is the day the library is closed. The only place that we planned to start

I turned to face Aiden, who was already looking at me. "What do we do?"

Aiden's gaze shifted from me to the closed library doors and then back again. He sighed before responding, "It looks like we have no other choice."

"What?" I asked, tilting my head.

"My house it is."

—

Word count: 1900

09 | Miller's sanctuary

- -

I'm currently seated in Aiden's car. We decided, and by we, I mean mostly him, to do it at his house.

15 minutes ago

"You're kidding, right?" I said, my voice tinged with disbelief.

Miller's deadpan expression remained unchanged as he replied. "Does this look like a situation for me to be joking, Thompson?"

I scanned the surroundings, desperately searching for alternative solutions, but my mind drew a blank. Defeated, I reluctantly nodded.

"Okay, but just for today. Next time, we need to find a solution that doesn't involve going to anyone's house." I firmly say.

I watched as a small smile formed on his face before he nodded in agreement. "Yes, ma'am" he responded obediently.

With a heavy sigh, we made our way towards the parking lot, knowing that there was no other choice.

—

The atmosphere was quiet, with the only sound being the wind blowing. God, this was awkward; this is my first time being in his car. Each passing minute felt like an eternity as we drove through the streets. Going further and further away from school

Never before had I imagined finding myself in this position—sitting beside Aiden in his fucking car. Our paths had never really crossed outside of school, but yet here we were, me in his car, driving to his house.

Oh God, I blame this on Miss Marsha.

I scan around; the car wasn't bad at all; the interior was clean and organized, which is surprising to me knowing that this is Aiden's car after all; and the leather of the seats was blue, which is a colour I noticed that Aiden loves. The car was really nice; I can give that to him.

"Like the ride?" His voice broke me out of my thoughts, and I glanced to my left. Where he was seated, our gaze met for a second.

"Hm, not bad" I respond, crossing my arms and nodding.

He let out a low chuckle, shaking his head. As I watched him drive, I couldn't help but notice the way he did it. His posture is straight,with one hand confidently gripping the steering wheel while the other rested casually on the window ledge. As he guided his hand along the wheel, I couldn't help but notice the veins that snaked their way across his hand and up his arm. They seemed to pulse with every turn of the wheel.

I know this may sound weird, but that was kind of attractive.

I quickly shook my head, turning my eyes straight in front of me and focusing on the road. I was not about to think of that again.

5 minutes later

The car pulled up. In his driveway, the house was big, and when I say big, I mean huge. It had a spacious and imposing structure with multiple levels, maybe four and a grand entrance. The exterior of the house was adorned with elegant details and large windows that allowed plenty of natural light to enter.

The house featured a front yard with lush green grass and neatly trimmed hedges. A paved pathway led from the driveway to the front entrance.

Wow, I knew he was rich, but not this rich.

After he parked, he leaned in, unbuckling my seatbelt with a smile. "We're here, sweetheart."

We hoped out and started making our way inside.

I took a deep breath. Before we entered,The inside was just as big; we were greeted in a spacious foyer with high ceilings and a grand staircase leading upstairs. The walls were adorned with artwork and family portraits.

I noticed most of them had someone that looked similar to Aiden, but Aiden wasn't in most of them. hm strange

As we made our way through the room, my eyes caught sight of a small portrait hanging on the wall. It was a picture of Aiden, but he looked much younger in it. I couldn't help but let out a snicker at the sight.

"Wait, is that you?" I blurted out, unable to contain my amusement.

Aiden stopped in his tracks, his expression shifting from surprise to a cocky smile. He turned to face me "Yes, looking cute like always"

I roll my eyes in response. "You were way cuter back then, maybe even less annoying."

A playful glimmer danced in his eyes as he queried, "So you think I'm cute?" Aiden said ignoring the last part of my comment

"Oh, please" was all I could say, trying to hide my true thoughts. I mean, it was obvious that Aiden was attractive, like very attractive, but I wasn't going to admit that. If those words came out of my mouth, it would only lead to endless teasing and embarrassment.

Aiden smirked at my response and then proceeded to lead me upstairs. The upstairs area of his house was incredibly spacious, with rooms scattered in every corner of the walls.

"We're going to study in my room, alright?"

I reluctantly nodded, not particularly thrilled about the idea, but I'm already at his house, and that's already bad enough.

The atmosphere in Aiden's room was serene and inviting; his room was very spacious and looked two times the size of my living room. I don't know how that's even possible. His room doesn't have a lot of furniture, just his huge king-size bed, a desk, and other little things.

The room had a dark layout, but it still looked inviting. On his shelf, I noticed a display of all his trophies from his football games and academic awards. Of course, he had them on full display.

"Uh, where should I sit?" I asked nervously while playing with my fingers. This was my first time ever being in a boy's room, and what makes it worse is that it's in Aiden's room.

This is my first time, and in Aiden's room. God

"We'll sit over there" he said, motioning at his huge desk. The desk, like the rest of the room, was well organized and tidy, with only a few essential items scattered across its surface.

Noticing my obvious nervous demeanour, a smirk appeared on Aiden's face.

"Why so nervous, first time being in a man's room?" He teased, his voice tinged with amusement.

I felt my cheeks flush as I tried to compose myself, unsure of how to respond. "Shut up, Miller."

He chucked, "I'm going to change to something more comfortable, see y'a."

With that, he left, and I was left here alone in his room. Oh God, what did I put myself into? I went to sit on his desk, placing my bag beside me.

A couple of minutes later, Aiden came out. He was wearing grey sweats, paired with a black compression-like t-shirt, that accentuated his body, even revealing hints of his abs.This was my first time ever seeing him outside of his uniform, and he looked-

"Took you long enough" I muttered, averting my gaze momentarily.

"Sorry, ma'am" he replied sarcastically.

"Anyways, let's just get this over with. Come on."I said as I was taking out my laptop and papers.

Aiden took a seat across from me, his gaze never leaving mine. Sensing his intense gaze, I looked up and caught him staring. "What is it?"

With a smile playing on his lips, Aiden averted his gaze momentarily before responding. "Oh, nothing"

I could tell he wanted to say something.

"Spit it out, Miller." I urged

He hesitated for a moment before finally revealing his thoughts. "I just never thought that you, of all people, would be in my room, let alone be the first person to step foot in here."

I tilted my head, intrigued by his words. "The first person?" I repeated

Aiden nodded slowly, his gaze still locked on mine. "Yes" he confirmed. "Whenever I bring people over, my room is strictly off-limits."

I wanted to ask him why but stopped, knowing that it wasn't really my place to know.

An awkward silence hung in the air; it's as if he unwillingly revealed a part of him that no one knew. I mean, who would have guessed that Aiden Miller has never brought anyone into his room? Not me

As we sat there in silence, the unspoken understanding between us grew stronger.

—

Word count: 1384

10 | Total bust

2 years ago

"You two are one of our most exampled students in the academy. I do not want to see this behaviour ever again. You understand?"

"Yes, ma'am," we responded quietly, our voices barely audible.

"What did I say?" She demanded

"Yes, ma'am!" We replied in unison loudly this time.

The stern gaze of our teacher bore down on us as she spoke, her words laced with disappointment. "Good. Now, think about your actions while you clean the classroom. You two will be on cleaning duty for the next two weeks." With that, she turned and briskly exited the room, leaving behind the echo of a slamming door.

I swiftly turned to face Aiden, my frustration evident in my expression. "This is all your fault, Miller," I accused, my voice tinged with exasperation. "Because of you, we're stuck on cleaning duty."

He purred his lips while rolling his eyes. "I didn't even do anything." He resorted defensively: "You're the one who hit him. I gave you a warning."

I rolled my eyes, groaning, "Warning, my ass, this is all your fault. So you have to clean the room by yourself."

I handed Aiden the broom, observing as he glanced at it and then back at me, raising an eyebrow in disbelief. "Please," he retorted, handing the broom back to me, "you did it; you clean up."

"You're such a repulsive, abominable vermine."

"Oh wow, congratulations! Did you just learn those words today?" He joked with a laugh.

I groan, running my hand through my hair. If you're wondering why we're here, It all started during our PE class when Aiden and I were paired together for a game of volleyball. As the game progressed, we got caught up in the moment, and things took a bad turn.

Long story short, the ball went soaring through the air and ended up colliding with the principal's face, causing his wig to fly off dramatically. In front of everybody

Yes, I know, that sounded very bad, and it was, so here we are stuck on cleaning duties for two weeks as our punishment.

"You're making this very hard for the both of us, Miller."

"No, you are." He replied

I inhaled deeply, then exhaled, "You know what, Miller, fine. Let's just both do it. I'll do this side; you do the other, got it?" I say, giving him a thumbs up.

"Yes, ma'am," he replied sarcastically.

5 minutes later

"God, this is tiring. How long has it been?"

"It's been five minutes, Miller." I deadpanned, rolling my eyes.

"Fuck," he whispered to himself, shaking his head in disbelief.

Yeah, we wouldn't be here if his dumbass wasn't playing around. This isn't actually the first time we got in trouble for doing something.

I'm always stuck in between the messes that he causes.

"Well, if you weren't such a dumbass," I muttered under my breath.

"What'd you say? dumbass?"

"Yes, that's what I said, wasn't it?" I respond annoyed.

"You're the one who couldn't catch a simple ball."

Slamming my broom on the floor in exasperation, I countered, "Simple? You'd sent that ball flying at me at full speed. How was I supposed to catch that?"

After that, you probably guessed what happened. We started bickering for the rest of the time and didn't get anything done. Which made our cleaning duties drag on for an additional week.

Now

As you can see, Aiden and I don't go together, especially when it comes to working together; things don't always go right.

"Miller, can you please sit down so we can finally start?" I glanced over at him, sprawled on his bed, casually tossing a small football into the air. His well-defined muscles were noticeable as he turned towards me with a sigh. "I can't find the motivation to start this project," he admitted. "When is it due again?"

"By the end of this month."

He let out a soft "hm" as he continued tossing the ball in the air.

"Miller," I groan. "What can I do to make you start?"

He paused his ball-tossing and turned towards me, his hazel eyes locking onto mine. "You shouldn't ask questions like that, sweetheart," he said softly.

I let out an exasperated sigh. "Just answer my question; I want to get this project over with."

"Okay, okay" He chuckled, his tone teasing. "How about you sit beside me in class for one more month?"

"You really know how to torture me, Miller." I thought about it for a moment, then, with a nod of agreement, I urged him to sit so that we could start.

Responding to my request with a sly smile, he eagerly rose from his bed, stretching his body. As he extended his arms, the fabric of his shirt shifted, briefly revealing the subtle contours of his abs.

This guy has a way of making his abs visible. I know he did it on purpose, with the sly smile he currently has on his face.

I sighed as he finally sat back on his seat, beside me this time.

—

"No, no, no! Ew, that one was even worse than the last three," I exclaimed with a hint of frustration.

"Thompson," he let out with a sigh.

"They all suck." I couldn't help but shudder with a disgusted look on my face.

"All of these templates look the exact same," he added while running his hand through his hair.

"No, the fonts are different, which makes a huge difference." I corrected

He shook his head. "You're just indecisive."

"Nope, how the template looks is very important."

"We've spent the last ten minutes searching for a template when we could've started the project." Aiden lamented

"Don't blame this on me; you wasted most of the time by throwing that ball in the air for like fifteen minutes."

"You're impossible; you know that."

I shot back, "Same goes to you."

Before we could continue our little banter, the sound of a door opening interrupted us.

I quickly moved away from Aiden, realizing how close we were.

He sighed, "Hi mom."

—

"It's been such a while since we last met, and you've blossomed into a beautiful young lady," Aiden's mother exclaimed, her face glowing with delight.

She looked a bit older; from the last time we met, her hair was still black but with tiny hints of grey, and her eyes were still beautiful with that mesmerizing hazel colour, one similar to Aiden's.

Checking the time, I realized it was time for me to take my leave. "Well, I should start heading out now. It was lovely to meet you, miss," I politely stated.

With a curious tilt of her head she offered, "Oh, you can call me Madelyn. Are you absolutely certain you don't want to stay for dinner?"

"No, thank you. I really must be on my way."

Aiden came out of his closet while putting a sweater over his head. "Let me drive you home, then."

—

When we started driving, the sun began its descent, casting a warm glow across the horizon.

The atmosphere was filled with undeniable tension, a lingering reminder of how our previous encounter ended. Today had been a complete disappointment; we did absolutely nothing, thanks to both Aiden and a bit of myself too. I can admit my own fault.

As the sun gradually disappeared below the horizon, its rays danced upon our faces.

I couldn't help but notice Aiden's reaction as he instinctively shielded his eyes from the light. In that moment, the sun accentuated his features, making them more pronounced and captivating.

His dark raven hair framed his face, while his deep hazel eyes sparkled with allure. His dark eyebrows furrowed slightly, adding an air of intensity to his countenance. It was moments like these when Aiden truly revealed his beauty, and I found myself realizing just how attractive he truly was.

Well, mostly because he's not opening his mouth or smirking at every chance he gets.

"Zhera." The deep sound of my name brought me out of my trance.

I let out a soft "yes." I almost whispered. This was one of the few times Aiden had said my name. I can't even remember the other ones.

"When should we do it again?" he inquired, briefly glancing in my direction. I pondered his question for a moment before replying."Ah, how about after tomorrow? I'm kind of busy tomorrow."

He let out a soft "mhm", as he deftly manoeuvred the car onto my street. As the car came to a halt in front of my house, I started to gather my things.

"See y'a ," he said with a slight wave.

Returning the gesture, I waved back before gracefully exiting the vehicle. When I finally made my way inside the house, I heard the faint sound of a car driving off.

—

This chapter was pretty fun to write. Tell me your honest opinions.

wordcount: 1491

11 | Poison

These past two days, I have stayed home. I suddenly got a fever out of the blue. I guess it came yesterday, when I was outside for practically the whole day, preparing for the upcoming event at school.

God. The timing of this fever could not have been worse; there is so much to do as the student council president, plus the loads of assignments I have, and most importantly, that shitty project in science that counts like so much of my grade.

Fuck, I hate this so much. My whole body is aching, I'm sweating so much, and I have a very bad headache. I just want to end it all.

Feeling overwhelmed and frustrated, I called out to my mom, shouting as loudly as I could.

However, to my dismay, I was met with complete silence, realizing that she wasn't home. This only added to my distress; I was left to suffer alone with my fever. Tears started rolling down my eyes.

The loud ringing of my phone broke me out of my breakdown. I groggily reached out to answer it, hoping it was mom calling to check in on me.

Looking at the caller, I let out an audible groan, tilting my head back.

"What is it?"

"Hello, to you too," Aiden said, his voice dripping with sarcasm.

I let out a cough before sniffing my nose. "I don't feel good; get to your point."

"Open your door," he replied, his tone unwavering.

What. I stammered for a bit before finding the words, "What?"

"I said, Open your door. Thompson." His words hung in the air, leaving me even more perplexed. Was this some kind of joke?

I laughed, "You cannot be serious," then abruptly got off my bed and made my way towards the window. As I peered outside, there he was, standing on my doorstep, waving his hands with a huge smile on his face.

I quickly shut the blinds, taking my phone in my hand and saying, "Miller. What are you doing here?"

"Answer the door, and I'll tell you," he responded calmly.

"What if I said no?"

"Than I'll stay until your parents come home."

If my parents saw a boy waiting at the front door for me, I'd be dead, especially my dad. He's a pretty chill guy, but when it comes to boys, he does not play.

"Fuck," I quietly muttered under my breath, thinking about what I should do. Should I let him say it out there until he finally decides to leave, knowing he won't, or should I just let him in to see me in this state?

"No," I finally uttered, then ended the call quickly before he could respond.

I then crawled into bed and pulled the covers over my head.

However, my moment of peace was short-lived as my phone began to ring again. I ignored the calls, declining each one swiftly.

Eventually, the ringing ceased, and I was met with a blissful silence.

But just as I thought Aiden had finally given up and left, the sound of rocks hitting against my window shattered my thoughts.

Startled, I hurriedly opened the window, only to have a small rock hit me square on the forehead. "What the hell, Miller!" I exclaimed, while rubbing the spot.

"Sorry, sweetheart." He replied with a half-smile.

"Just go home; what are you even doing here?"

"Let me in, and I'll tell you."

Sighing, I hesitated for a moment, contemplating whether to let him in or not.

"If I let you in, you can only stay for a bit, just to explain to me why you're here, and then you'll leave, okay?"

He simply nodded.

Wrapping my blanket over my body, I headed downstairs.

—

"What is it?"

"You look like a mess." He pointed it out while trying to hold in a laugh.

"If you're here to insult me, you're welcome to leave." I said, trying to push him out.

He simply laughed. Knowing how my antics to push him were to no avail he stayed glued to the floor.

"Just tell me why you're here." I asked, after finally giving up and clearing my throat.

"Honestly, I have no idea." He ran his hand through his hair with a smile.

"Get out," I coldly said. Sniffling

Aiden shook his head. "You obviously have a cold, and I can't let that come between our projects, so I came to check up."

"Is that really why you're here?" I asked, raising my eyebrows.

He nodded. Alright, if he was here only because of the project, then I guess.

"Alright, let's just" I began to say, but my words were cut off by a sudden throbbing in my head. This fever was giving me the worst headaches. I instinctively placed my hand on my forehead, wincing in pain.

Aiden quickly pulled me back up.

"No, don't touch me; I'm sick," I said, trying to distance myself from him.

He shook his head, a smile on his face. "I've been standing close to you for the past minutes; that's already done."

I sighed, leaning against the wall, still feeling the effects of the fever. It was a relief to have someone here with me while I'm sick, but at the same time, it's Aiden. I'd rather anyone else then Aiden Miller.

I shook my head. "You should go; I'm fine."

"Fine?" he questioned, raising his voice. "You're burning up."

He was right. I could feel my face heating up, and I didn't want him to see me like this, all red and sick. In fact, I didn't want anyone to see me like this.

Aiden led me to the couch and gently made me sit down. "Sit over here".

I watched as he started to walk away, and instinctively, I called out, "Where are you going?"

"Kitchen."

—

I lay on the couch, my breathing labored, my body burning with heat, and my nose completely stuffed. I felt incredibly uncomfortable, especially with Aiden in my house conducting some sort of experiment in my kitchen.

After a few minutes, he emerged with a drink in his hands and a proud smirk on his face. The smell wafted towards me, and I wrinkled my nose in disgust. Even though the drink wasn't close to me, I could already detect its pungent aroma. What on earth was in that cup?

"Ew, what is that?" I asked, my voice laced with disgust.

"Drink this and don't argue with me."

"No," I countered, deciding to argue. "That substance will not enter my body."

He shook his head, seemingly amused. "Come on, it's not that bad."

"Whatever that is looks like a potion that is used to poison someone."

"Thompson,"

"Miller," I replied, crossing my arms and raising an eyebrow.

"Even when you're sick, you're still your stubborn self," he chuckled.

"I'm not stubborn," I insisted. "Just look at what you're holding and tell me it's not something they used in the 1800s to poison someone. There are literal bubbles floating out of it."

Aiden laughed, shaking his head. "It's not that bad, look." He took a sip, trying to prove his point.

His face scrunched up—well, there's an expression I've never seen on him. He quickly swallowed the drink, coughing for a bit. Before turning around and flashing me a smile.

"See, it's awesome."

I couldn't help but giggle. "If awesome is the new word for disgusting, then you're absolutely right."

"I'll just leave it here, and you can decide whether you want to give it a try and feel better or continue suffering here for days," he said, walking back to the kitchen.

Left alone, I pondered whether I should take a chance and drink it. With a deep breath, I grabbed the bottle and started chugging the entire drink, my hands pressed firmly against my nose.

Oh God, it is poison.

— ah, the sick trope, how I love it so much ;)

wordcount: 1328

12 | Care

The taste was still lingering in my throat—a disgusting taste. I swear Aiden tried to seriously poison me. The mere thought of it sent shivers down my spine.

"Thompson"

I refused to acknowledge him, crossing my arms defiantly as I stared straight ahead.

A moment passed, and then another, as silence settled between us like a heavy fog. It was in this silence that I could feel Aiden's gaze burning into the side of my face, his impatience palpable.

"Come on, Thompson," he pleaded. "When are you going to talk to me?"

When you apologize for trying to poison me.

"Is it because of the drink?"

I nodded, sniffling my nose.

"It wasn't that bad," he whispered.

I snapped, "It wasn't that bad? I passed out for two minutes."

Aiden quickly interrupted, correcting me, "Actually, it was only one minute and a half."

I gave him a skeptical look. "Fine, one and a half minutes. But seriously, what the hell was in that cup?"

Aiden furrowed his brows. "I'd rather not say."

He then burst into laughter as I let out an exasperated groan and sank deeper into the cozy embrace of my couch. "You know, for someone who claims to be trying to make me feel better, you're doing a pretty good job of the opposite."

He chuckled, his grin widening. "Hey, but it worked, didn't it? You're feeling a bit better now, right?"

I nodded, a reluctant smile tugging at the corners of my lips. "Yeah, I guess whatever that was did the trick."

—

The air between us hung heavy with an unusual silence, one that felt strangely comforting rather than awkward or uncomfortable.

Although the sun was on the verge of setting, its warm glow still illuminated the room, creating a calm atmosphere.

The gentle hum of the fan provided a soothing background noise, occasionally interrupted by my own coughs and sniffles.

This was the first time I actually felt okay in the presence of Aiden. But his existence still irked me.

He lounged on the couch, spreading his legs without a care, as if he owned the place, even though this was Aiden's first time coming to my house. His vacant gaze seemed fixed on some distant point, lost in thoughts I could only speculate about. He's probably thinking of a new way to poison me.

"So you know about the football game that's coming up?"

I turned my gaze towards him, shaking my head in response.

"Our team is going up against St.August; are you coming?"

I shrugged, "No idea; not really my scene."

He repositioned himself, placing his hands behind his head. "Well, you should come; it's going to be good."

"You're saying that as if you know for sure that our team is going to win."

A grin appeared on his face as he confidently said, "We will win; trust me. After all, you're sitting in front of the best player in the school." I couldn't help but scoff at his audacity.

"Alright, I'll consider it," I conceded, and a satisfied smile spread across his face.

"Wait, pass me your phone for a second."

"Why?"

"I have to look something up since my phone is dead."

I reluctantly handed it over to him, a hint of suspicion in my eyes.

He leaned in and started typing, a small smirk forming on his lips. "Miller, you better not be doing some nonsense on my phone."

He looked up at me, his expression innocent. "No, just looking something up. Alright, done. Thanks."

He handed me back my phone, but this time, his smirk had grown bigger. I couldn't help but wonder what he had done, but I decided to trust him for now.

I let out a tired sigh as I pushed myself off the couch, my limbs protesting after laying down for so long. With a groan, I began stretching my back, desperately trying to alleviate some of the stiffness.

Turning to face Aiden. "Aiden, I think you should go home now; my dad will be home soon."

"How about I wait for him? I want to say hi to the old man."

I shook my head, a mix of concern and frustration in my voice. "You can't be serious! If my dad sees you here, you're, Well, let's just say it won't end well."

But before I could finish my sentence, the sound of keys jingling pierced the air. My heart skipped a beat. Why on earth was my dad home so early? Panic washed over me as I realized the situation I was in. "Oh no."

As the front door swung open, I felt like I was standing on the edge of a precipice. It was as if I had dug my own grave and now had to face the consequences.

As my dad's deep, croaky voice filled the room, I couldn't help but feel a sense of unease. "Zhera, I'm home," he announced.

I mustered up the courage to respond, my voice barely above a whisper. "Hi, Dad," I greeted him quietly.

"Hi honey," he replied without looking at me, placing his coat and keys on the hanger.

Out of nowhere, Aiden chimed in with a friendly greeting. "Hello, Mister Thompson," he said, his voice breaking the tense silence. He just had to open that big mouth of his.

My dad stopped in his tracks. turning around slowly, his face filled with confusion. "Who is this?"

Panicking, I stumbled over my words as I tried to explain. "Uh, Dad, this is Aiden Miller. He came here for our project, the one I've been telling you about," I stammered.

"You two couldn't have found another place?"

"No, sir, the library at school is closed, so we couldn't go there. And since Zhera is sick, I decided to check up on her."

My dad's expression softened a bit as he seemed to recognize the name. "You're Aiden Miller? Madelyne's son," he said. "It's been a while since I saw you. Nice to meet you."

Aiden smiled and walked towards my dad, extending his hand for a handshake. "It's nice to meet you too, sir," he said politely.

I stood there, blinking in disbelief at the turn of events. My dad, who had always been strict with boys, was now shaking hands with Aiden. It was as if I had entered an alternate reality. This couldn't be my dad. It had to be some sort of clone, right?

"How's your family doing?" My dad asked

"We're alright, thank you."

My dad smiled, "You should go take a seat; my wife is coming soon. I know she would like to greet; it's been a while."

I gasped as I heard him say mom's coming."Mom's coming soon?" I repeated

"Yes, she'll be here in a couple of minutes."

I nodded slowly. The thought of momcoming soon made my heart race.
Unlike my dad, she wasn't as strict when it came to boys, but she did have
her concerns about them being a distraction from my studies. I couldn't
help but feel a bit nervous about how she would react to Aiden.

—

"Aiden, it's been years since we last met." My mom happily said this while
hugging Aiden. "You've grown into such a handsome man; last time I saw
you, you were this small. How are you doing?"

Aiden smiled. "I'm doing great, thank you."

"That's nice. Oh, have you eaten yet?"

He shook his head.

Without hesitation, my mom insisted, "Oh, you must stay for dinner! I
can't let you leave on an empty stomach, can I?"

A quiet groan escaped my lips as I muttered, "Mom." Spending half the day
with Aiden was one thing, but now he was being invited to stay for dinner?
Oh God.

Gently shushing me, my mom explained, "He's hungry, honey, and I can't
let him leave like this." With that, she led Aiden towards the dining room,
leaving me to contemplate the evening.

Aiden turned to me with a playful smile on his face. "Yeah, Zhera, I'm
hungry," he teased.

Fuck my life.

—

wordcount: 1350

13 | Dinner

"No way, he's at your house."

"Yes, he is." I whispered angrily, pacing around my room.

Ciara couldn't contain her excitement. "So you're telling me you have one of the hottest guys that we know in your house?"

"And you're complaining? Girl, you better appreciate the situation!" Kehlani chimed in; I could just imagine her waving her hands in the air as she spoke.

I pursed my lips, trying to downplay the situation. "Guys, it's not just any guy. It's Aiden Miller."

"Yeah, yeah, your rival or whatever," Ciara teased, not realizing how much that word made me cringe.

"Ew, don't call him my rival. That's cringe," I retorted. "anyways, the thing is, he's been at my house for like half the day."

The line went quiet for a second

"Half the day!?" they both screamed in unison.

"Wait, wait, wait, so you were alone with him for half the day?" Ciara questioned

"Uh, yes?"

"Wow, Z, I didn't know you were like that," Kehlani teased.

I scrunched my face. "What do you mean?"

Kehlani continued, "Staying home alone with a guy. That's not something Zhera Thompson would do."

"Oh, shut up," I retorted, attempting to hide the slight embarrassment that crept up within me. Kehlani's words had hit a nerve, making me question whether I was becoming too predictable or if I had lost touch with the fun side of myself.

Ciara chuckled in the background, "Well, good luck." "I gotta go; my mom's calling me." She then hung up.

"Well, I think you're lucky, Z"

I scoffed "Of course you would say that, Keh."

She laughed. "I mean, if I had a guy who looked like that, that was staying at my house, I would not complain."

I couldn't help but laugh along with her. "Stop! I'm in distress here! What if-" Before I could finish my sentence, I heard my name being called from downstairs.

"Sorry, Keh, Mom's calling me. See you tomorrow," I quickly said, ending the call.

I placed my phone down on the table, a heavy sigh escaping my lips. I felt a mix of nervousness coursing through my veins.

With hurried steps, I made my way out of the room, my mind racing with thoughts and emotions. However, in my haste, I bumped into something—or someone.

Looking up slowly, I rolled my eyes as I recognized Aiden standing before me. He had that mischievous glint in his eyes that always managed to irritate me.

Without missing a beat, he placed his hand around my shoulder and lightly pulled me away from him.

"Thompson" he said, a smirk playing on his lips.

"Miller."

He peered down at me for what seemed like an eternity, his gaze piercing through mine. I held his stare, refusing to break eye contact.

"You look better," he finally said.

I shrugged. "Yeah, I guess my immune system is just that good."

Aiden chuckled softly, his laughter filling the space between us. "I guess it was. Now shall we go eat?"

I grumbled under my breath and started making my way downstairs with him.

The smell of food wafted through the air, and the atmosphere felt warm and welcoming. Calming music played on the TV, and the fireplace added to the cozy ambiance. It was a lively scene, unlike anything I had seen in this house before.

As we made our way downstairs, I noticed my dad tidying up his desk, and my mom was bustling in the kitchen. I called out, "Yes, Mom?"

"Make the table for me, please." I hummed, trying to gather the plates, and stood on my tiptoes to grab them.

"I got it," Aiden said swiftly, taking the plates from his hands. Before I could even grasp them, he gave me a playful wink. I couldn't help but roll my eyes. show off.

We started making the table, and dinner was ready.

"So, Aiden, I heard you play football?" my dad asked, wiping his mouth with a handkerchief.

Aiden nodded. "Yes, sir. I've been playing since I started high school."

"Are you planning on pursuing it at a higher level after high school?"

Aiden shook his head and said, "No, it's just a hobby for me. I don't want to take it too seriously." I was surprised to hear that. I always thought Aiden would want to play in college.

"Wow, most athletes go on to play professionally after high school. I guess you're more focused on your academics."

"Yes, sir," Aiden confirmed.

An awkward silence suddenly filled the room, with only the clattering of plates breaking the stillness. This is what I had feared. Dinner was usually awkward and quiet, but now with a guest, it felt twice as uncomfortable.

My mom cleared her throat and changed the subject. "I heard you guys have an important project. How's it going?"

"Well, we've started it, but we still have a lot of research to do." I replied.

"Yeah, I wonder why," Aiden muttered under his breath, making sure only I could hear.

I quickly reacted by discreetly stepping on his foot under the table. He winced, his mouth twitching to suppress a reaction.

My mom, oblivious to the silent exchange, continued, "I hope you both do well and bring home excellent grades."

I smiled sweetly and said, "Yeah." Even with guests around, my mom still brings up grades. I shouldn't be surprised anymore.

"You guys are free to do it here for as long as you like, until the library is repaired," my mom offered.

My dad glanced at her for a moment before returning his attention to his food. It was clear he didn't like the idea.

"Thank you, but I'm pretty sure the repairs were just for a couple of days. They'll probably be done by tomorrow," Aiden expressed, attempting to ease the tension.

"Alright," she replied.

Just as the atmosphere began to settle, Aiden's phone started ringing. He quickly excused himself.

I could hear snippets of the conversation from his phone, and it seemed urgent. "Alright, mom. I'll be there," Aiden said, a sense of urgency in his voice.

I couldn't help but smile. It sounded like he had to leave soon, which meant I would have some time to myself.

Aiden hurriedly returned to the table and finished his food. "Thank you for the meal. It was delicious. But I have to leave now. Something important came up," he trailed off.

"Alright, take care. Zhera, take him out," I groaned quietly, muttering a barely audible "sure" under my breath.

As we made our way towards the door, I swung it open wide "Well, it looks like this is where we part ways."

Aiden, with a smug smile, leaned close "I could use a thank you before I leave."

I raised an eyebrow. "For what?"

"Thompson."

"Miller."

He leaned in even closer, his confidence evident. "Well, it looks like you're all better now. I'm an amazing caretaker, right?"

"Sure you are, Miller," I replied, crossing my arms. I guess he is; I feel way better now. I don't think I would've felt like this if he hadn't come over.

"Bye, sweetheart," he smiled before stepping out the door. I simply waved, a light smile gracing my face.

Closing the door behind me, I leaned against it, letting out a sigh. Maybe I should have thanked him? I mean, he did make me feel better. But at the end of the day, he's still the typical Aiden—the one who knows how to push my buttons and make me mad.

When I opened my eyes, I saw my dad standing in front of me. With a look on his face

"yes?"

He simply raised his eyebrows and smiled, then walked away.

—

wordcount: 1294

14 | Preparations

"Man, I can't wait for the football game!" Khelani exclaimed with a huge grin on her face.

"Totally! It feels like forever since we had one at school," Ciara replied, sharing Khelani's excitement.

I closed my locker with a tired sigh and rubbed my eyes. "Wait, you guys are actually going to the game?"

"Of course! And you're coming with us, Zhe," they both chimed in.

I groaned. "Should I? I mean, it's not really my thing."

Ciara playfully squished my cheeks, declaring, "We're going to make it your thing, trust me!"

I grinned, "Alright, alright. Let's just hit up the washroom before class. I seriously need to fix this hot mess of a look."

As we strolled towards the washroom, I caught sight of the mirror and hurriedly made my way over.

"Leigha, are you going to go for it?" I overheard someone ask.

"Yeah, I hope Aiden digs it" a soft voice replied.

My curiosity piqued. I looked up and realized it was Leigha Windsor, one of the cheerleaders. She's known all over the school for her looks and most importantly because her family funds this school.

"I'm planning to give it to him during the football game tomorrow. Fingers crossed, he's into it," she whispered shyly.

"Leigha, he's going to be all over it. You're drop-dead gorgeous and super sweet," her friend reassured, giving her a comforting rub on the back.

"I'm just so nervous, you know? There are tons of girls asking him out. What makes me stand out?"

Her friend let out a sigh and said, "Aiden's a good guy, so don't expect the worst. Just go for it, alright?"

Just as the bell rang, they hurried off.

Both Ciara and Khelani exchanged a knowing glance before letting out a scoff. I furrowed my brows in confusion.

"What's going on?" I asked

Khelani raised both eyebrows and smirked. "Good luck with that" she said, her tone filled with amusement.

I looked at her, still puzzled. "What do you mean?"

Ciara jumped in to clarify. "What we're trying to say is that Aiden has turned down every single girl who has ever asked him out. It's like a known fact."

I tilted my head, genuinely surprised. "Really? I had no idea."

Thinking about it I never saw that cocky bastard with a girl, or like a girlfriend. He did sometimes talk about how girls are all over him but never said he had a girlfriend.

They exchanged another look, and Ciara shook her head with a playful smile. "And that's why we say you live under a rock."

I shrugged. "I just don't pay much attention to that kind of stuff. Besides, why would I care about Aiden's love life?"

They both nodded, giving me a look.

—

"Alright, class," the teacher announced. "Today, we will be continuing our work from yesterday. Please pair up with the person sitting beside you and continue where you left off."

I turned my gaze to my right, meeting the blue eyes of Michael. We both stared at each other awkwardly. I mean, how awkward is it to talk to the boy your friend is seeing?

"Uh, so I wasn't here yesterday; could you tell me what you guys did?"

A faint smile appeared on his face as he responded, "Sure, no problem. We started working on this paper, but now we have to finish it." He handed me a sheet of paper. "Here, use this."

"Thanks," I replied, accepting the paper from him. "So, I'll start working on it, and when I reach the part where you left off, we can continue together. Does that sound alright?"

He nodded in agreement and focused his attention on his own paper. I followed suit and began working on my assignment.

I suddenly felt someone look at me and turn to my right, catching Michael staring. I raised an eyebrow, then he quickly looked away.

Um, what was that? I hate when people stare, and him of all people makes it very awkward.

Michael cleared his throat, initiating a conversation. "So, Zhera, right?" he asked.

I nod, briefly taking my eyes off my paper.

"I noticed you weren't here for the past couple of days. Are you feeling better now?"

I smile and say, "I was just sick."

As I continued working on my paper, he suddenly asked, "Hey, I heard you're really smart. Do you think you could help me with math after school?"

I paused for a moment, scratching my head. "Hmm, I'm not sure. I have a lot on my plate with student council responsibilities. But I'll see."

His expression shifted briefly, a mix of disappointment and maybe even a hint of frustration. But he quickly masked it with a smile. "No worries, just let me know."

—

The bell rang, and I quickly got up, feeling annoyed with Michael for talking too much and not taking the hint that I wanted to focus on my work.

He started with small talk that didn't make sense, and I tried to subtly indicate that I wasn't interested in the conversation.

But despite my efforts, he took it as a sign to keep talking. Now I'm frustrated and have made no progress on my work.

I usually prefer to complete my assignments at school, so I don't have a lot of homework to do at home. However, today's interruption has left me with nothing done and a sour mood.

I sighed and slammed my locker shut, waiting for Ciara and Khelani to arrive. As part of our usual routine, we meet up at my locker after each class.

"Zhera, guess what?" Kehlani exclaimed, catching me off guard with her sudden appearance.

I couldn't help but wonder how she managed to get here so quickly, considering her class is on the other side of the school. But then again, it's Kehlani we're talking about—what kind of answer am I expecting? Maybe she teleported or something.

"What happened?"

She caught her breath. "So, there's this hot guy in my class. I never really noticed him before because he always sat at the back. But today, he spoke up, and let me tell you, he's smoking hot. I'm pretty sure his name is Alejandro."

Ah, Alejandro. That name rang a bell. He's one of Aiden's friends.

I couldn't help but tease Kehlani. "So, he's your new crush now, huh?" I already knew the answer but wanted to hear it from her.

Kehlani nodded enthusiastically. "Yeah, duh! I have to find a way to get closer to him; thankfully, he's in my class next period."

I chuckled, wishing her good luck. "Well, Khe, I wish you all the best of luck. May the forces of attraction be in your favour."

As I glanced at the time, I frowned. "shit. Sorry, Khe, but I have a student meeting right now. Please let Ciara know that I won't be in class with her today."

"Kk!"

—

I opened the door, out of breath. "Sorry guys, the hallways were so crowded."

"It's fine; we're just getting started."

With a smile, I made my way to my seat "So should we start planning for the homecoming dance?"

"Yes, but before we dive into that, we need to ensure that the preparations for the football game tomorrow are going well." Roman explained, perching his thick-rimmed rectangular glasses up properly.

Roman is the student council's secretary; he takes care of organizing events and distributing information to members.

I turned to Myvy, a girl standing beside Roman's chair. "Alright, so what do we have for now Myvy?"

She swiftly took out her note book. "Well, the tickets are finished, and we will be distributing them tomorrow. We have the numbers of students that will be attending and have planned everything for the parking."

I hummed, "So it looks like we have everything done for now. Good job."

A soft smile graced Myvy's face as she tucked her blonde hair behind her ear. As the event coordinator, she took care of brainstorming ideas and ensuring the smooth running of events.

A few moments later, the sound of the door opening interrupted our conversation."Sorry. I was busy."Nora explained making her way through the door

I rolled my eyes. Nora was the vice president, but it didn't seem like she took her role seriously.

"Like always," I muttered quietly under my breath. She caught my comment and shot me a dirty look, mocking me in return.

It was clear that ever since I had won the election for president, against her, she had developed a dislike for me and consistently attempted to undermine my position.

"Let's just get this over with." Nora declared with a fake smile plastered across her face. She forcefully slammed her bag onto the table.

Myvy and Roman gave each other a look. But decided to keep quiet. I wasn't going to

"Look, if you don't want to be here, you're free to leave. You're seriously ruining the mood."

She scoffed, "Calm the fuck down, Miss President."

"Language," Roman interjected firmly.

"Relax, I'm just in a bad mood."

"Yes, we all have bad days," I said calmly. "But that doesn't mean you should make everyone else's day bad too. We have so much work to do, and if you're going to show up late and just mope around, perhaps it's best if you find the exit."

"Whatever, I never wanted to be in this boring ass club anyway."she grabbed her bag and stormed towards the door, forcefully slamming the door behind her.

I sighed, rubbing my head.

"I never liked her, anyway." Myvy shrugged

—

Football game coming soon! I'm exited

wordcount: 1613

15 | Game day

The air is crisp and cool, with a slight breeze rustling through the air. The sky is overcast, casting a grey hue over the field. As we make our way to the stands, I can see my breath in the chilly air. The smell of freshly popped popcorn fills the stadium, tempting my taste buds.

I can hear the vendors shouting, "Get your hot popcorn here!" and "Cold drinks, get 'em while they're icy!"

I smiled. Everyone is bundled up in cozy jackets, scarves, and hats, trying to stay warm. The stands are filled with purple and white, which are the school's colours.

The cheerleaders are in full swing, performing their routines on the sidelines, while the mascot is doing flips all around the place.

The ticket booth is bustling with activity, with people lining up to buy their tickets and get into the game. I spotted Roman standing next to the booth, holding a chequebook, while Myvy stood beside him, giving me a friendly wave as soon as she saw me. I returned the gesture with a wave of my own.

"This is amazing, guys." Khelani squealed as she turned around excitedly.

I couldn't help but let out a deep sigh, a smile spreading across my face. This was truly amazing. I had never attended a football game before, always finding an excuse to skip the ones hosted by our school. However, in this moment, I realized just how much I had been missing out on.

As we found our spots on the bleachers, Ciara made a quick detour to grab some popcorn for all of us. I settled into my seat and let my eyes wander across the field.

"Looking for Aiden?" Kehlani perched beside me.

"No, I was just looking around." I stammered

"No need to lie, Zhera; look, he's right there."

I followed her pointed finger, and there he was, sitting on the sidelines.

Aiden's legs were bouncing up and down, his face etched with a serious expression as his eyes remained fixed on the field. His jersey clung to his body, accentuating his physique. His chest rose and fell slowly as he immersed himself in the moment.

Suddenly, our eyes locked, and I blinked. This was the first time we saw each other since he was at my house. His expression immediately changed, the corners of his lips curling up.

Aiden gracefully rose from his seat and waved in my direction, prompting a chorus of excited squeals from the girls surrounding me.

"Oh my, he's waving over here!" one girl exclaimed, fanning her face.

"I know. Do you think he's waving at me?" Another girl whispered with hopeful excitement.

"Please, he's definitely waving at me," a third girl chimed in confidently.

I lightly waved back at him. Aiden mouthed the words, "You're all better now," and I nodded in agreement. With a mischievous twinkle in his eye, he raised his thumbs up and accompanied it with a playful wink.

I couldn't help but roll my eyes at his antics while the girls around me erupted into squeals.

"Why's everyone squealing like a bunch of pigs?" Ciara said as she handed us our popcorn. Sitting down beside Khelani

Suddenly, the crowd quiets down, indicating that the game is about to start. The players start to warm up as the coaches are talking.

"Oh, it looks like it's starting." Kehlani said, pinching my arm. I wince, slapping her buttery fingers off.

The wind cuts through the air, causing a gentle whistle that adds to the atmosphere. The players take the field, their breath forming small clouds as they finish warming up.

The sound of the referee's whistle pierces through the silence, signalling the start of the game. The first kickoff sends a collective cheer echoing through the stands, mingling with the crisp autumn breeze.

I could see Aiden swarming through the field as he caught the ball. Even though he had the same uniform as everyone else, he still stood out, mostly because of the big number 1 behind his jersey.

I know he forced the school to give him one.

As the first half drew to a close, neither team managed to score. The players made their way to the sides.

Aiden swiftly removed his helmet, vigorously shaking his head to free himself from its confines. Beads of sweat cascaded down his face, and he reached for his shirt to wipe away the moisture, inadvertently revealing his chiselled abs.

The sight elicited an eruption of excitement from the stands, with high-pitched squeals filling the air. I could see him smirking; he definitely did that on purpose.

"This guy knows what he's doing." Kehlani said while fanning herself with a whistle.

I shook my head, muttering,Cocky bastard."

I glanced to my right, noticing Ciara's silence. "What's the matter, C?".

"Oh, it's nothing. I just have to take this phone call," Ciara replied, her tone slightly distracted.

"Make it quick; the next match is about to start." Kehlani exclaimed as she took a huge chuck of Ciara's popcorn.

Ciara shot her a glare, and I laughed.

"God, it's freezing," I muttered, rubbing my hands together.

"I told you to wear something heavier, but no, you wanted to look all cute and fashionable. Now look where it got you," Kehlani scoffed, adjusting her huge puffer jacket snugly around her.

"Sorry, mom," I responded sarcastically, rolling my eyes. Just then, my phone rang. What a coincidence.

I excused myself. "Hello?"

"Where are you, young lady?"

—

make sure to like and vote!

wordcount; 925

16 | Final round

"Mom, what do you mean?" I stammered as I stood behind the stands, pulling my sweater tightly around me.

"I said, Where are you, Zhera Estrella Thompson?" she repeated. Fuck, she used my full name. That's how you know she's mad.

"Mom, I'm at the football game at school, the one I told you about a couple of days ago, remember?"

"I do not remember you mentioning that," she responded, her tone stern.

I felt a sinking feeling in my chest. How could she not remember? I vividly remember telling her about it and her giving me permission to go.

I whined, "But mom, I did! You said yes. I vividly remember that moment."

"Young lady, this is what you do—lie and not prioritize your studies. This is not how I raised you."

I frowned, feeling a wave of sadness wash over me. It hurt to hear her accuse me of lying and not caring about my studies. That's like the number one thing I prioritize.

I knew deep down that I had been honest with her and had been working hard in school. But right now, it felt like all my efforts were being disregarded.

"Mom, I'm so-"

Before I could finish my sentence, the call ended abruptly, leaving me with an unfinished sentence hanging in the air.

I slowly put the phone down. taking a deep breath. I am not about to let her ruin my night, nope.

I wiped away any traces of frustration from my face and began making my way towards the stands, but before I could get too far, I heard a familiar voice. It was Ciara. "You said you were coming," she said, her tone filled with disappointment.

"I know, but you promised me, this isn't the first time you know." I'm guessing she's talking to Michael; she sounds hurt.

I heard her take a sharp breath and then abruptly end the call. "Fuck!" she cursed, rubbing her eyes.

I approached her. "Everything alright, C?"

Her eyes widened momentarily, but she quickly transformed her expression into a soft smile. "Yeah, let's head back," she replied, taking my hand and leading me through the bustling crowd.

Ciara always has a way to hide her emotions; it was hard to tell what she was actually thinking of and how she was feeling. The best I could do was listen and wait until she wants to talk.

"Where are you guys? You missed like half of the game. I was pretty lonely without you two." Kehlani pouted while chugging her soda.

Ciara rubbed her shoulders. " We just got caught up with something, what's happening?"

"Well" Kehlani began, "Aiden is about to kick the ball to whoever and if it makes it in, our team wins a point."

"I really don't get this game," I muttered under my breath. Suddenly the crowd erupted in cheers. I looked around, confused, but stood up like everyone else, clapping my hands.

"What happened?" I whispered to Ciara, and she shrugged her shoulders. "No idea."

—

"Now, this is it, folks. The final round is about to begin, and if our team can make it, the Tigers will emerge victorious!" The commentator's voice boomed through the microphone.

Can he calm the hell down? There's no reason for him to be screaming in a mic. Making him sound 10 times louder

As the teams took their positions, a hush fell over the crowd. The players were visibly tense, and the crowd mirrored that tension.

With the piercing sound of the whistle, the match started. However, it quickly became evident that the other team had the advantage.

"I have no idea what is happening, but this is so good!" I exclaimed, bouncing my legs up and down

The opposing team was on the verge of taking a shot, and if they succeeded, it would mean victory for them.

"Ladies and gentlemen, it appears that the Eagles have the advantage. If the Tigers can somehow find a way to intervene, it could be their last chance to turn the tide of the game."

In a swift moment, a player skillfully caught the ball, gliding through the field and effortlessly manoeuvring past the opposing players.

I narrowed my eyes, trying to make out who it was. "Is that Aiden?"

"I think it is."

He proceeded to pass the ball to his teammates, each one making progress, inching closer and closer to the opposing side of the field.

"Oh, ladies and gentlemen, it seems that the Tigers have gained the upper hand. All thanks to player number one," exclaimed the commentator.

The crowd erupted in thunderous cheers, growing louder and louder with each passing moment. My heart raced. I never knew that watching a football game could make me feel like this.

"This is the moment we've all been waiting for, folks. It all comes down to this. If the Tigers can make it in, it will be the final game."

The ball was launched into the air, and time seemed to slow down as everyone held their breath.

The eagles fought to intercept, aware that if the ball made it, they would lose.

Kehlani shook me vigorously, her screams reverberating in my ears.

The ball found its way into the hands of Aiden, and without missing a beat, he sprinted the final yards to the other side, securing victory for our team.

The atmosphere returned to normalcy, with screams filling the air as popcorn and drinks were tossed in celebration. The players gathered around Aiden, their roars echoing throughout the stadium.

"I have no idea what just happened, but we did it!" Ciara squealed

I stood there, completely frozen, unable to find the right words to express my awe.Suddenly, a finger snapped in front of me, bringing me back to reality. "Earth to Zhera?" Kehlani asked, lightly nudging me.

"Wow" was all I managed to utter, still overwhelmed by the turn of events.

Kehlani nudged me again with a mischievous glint in her eyes. "We told you it would be fun. How about showing your gratitude by buying me some popcorn?"

I playfully squeezed her cheeks, chuckling, "Not a chance."

Suddenly, voices caught our attention.

"Wait, what's happening over there?"

"Is that Leigha? Oh my gosh, she's walking towards Aiden."

"Is she going to ask him out?"

I quickly turned to see Leigha approaching Aiden.

She had something in her hands. It seemed like she was about to make a move, just as she had mentioned before. In the washroom

"Hey, the players are heading off the field. Let's go down there!" Khelani exclaimed, grabbing our hands eagerly.

I chuckled and gently tugged back, "Hold on, why the rush?"

As we made our way down, we noticed a swarm of girls surrounding the players, attempting to strike up conversations. "Be right back, guys," Khelani announced before making her way towards someone in particular.

Ciara glanced in the direction Khelani was heading and asked, "Is that Alejandro?"

"Yep, it's him."

Ciara scratched her head, while raising an eyebrow. "Since when were they a thing?"

It seemed like Khelani's plan to get closer to Alejandro had worked. One thing was for sure: when Khelani sets her mind on something, she always finds a way to make it happen. Her confidence is one of the things I admire about her and something I would love to have.

I glimpsed to my right where Aiden and Leigha were, my eyes widening when I saw her go in for a hug.

—

Guys please go easy on me, I know nothing about American football, so I just wrote based on a couple of games I saw on the internet.

Anyways what do you guys feel about Leigha?

wordcount: 1289

17 | Library

Aiden seemed uncomfortable as he gently pushed Leigha away by her shoulder. I couldn't bear to watch, so I turned my head, not wanting to witness the rejection.

"When I get home, I'm dead." I groan, remembering my mom and my last call.

Ciara glanced up from her phone. "Why?"

"She didn't want me to come, but I remember asking her for permission and her saying yes."

She shook her head. "Parents"

Suddenly, Ciara's attention shifted, and she smiled. "I gotta go; be right back" she said hurriedly before leaving.

What was that?

Suddenly, I heard a name that hadn't crossed my ears in a while—"Thompson."

Slowly turning around, I found myself face-to-face with Aiden.

"Miller." A smile graced his lips, his features illuminated by the dim light of place. His hazel eyes gleamed with warmth. His dark hair was disheveled, with strands sticking to his damp forehead.

"You weren't half bad on the field" I remarked, crossing my arms.

"Darling, just admit that I was extraordinary" he retorted with a smirk. His confidence is still very high.

I rolled my eyes. While tightening my sweater, it's further into the evening now, so the weather has gone down. I should've brought a jacket.

"Come here." He whispered, beckoning me with a gentle gesture.

"What is it?" I inquired, my breath catching slightly as he gently placed something around my shoulders. It was his jersey.

"You're shaking like crazy; I can't have you fall sick again."

I shook my head. "Thanks, but I'm about to go, so it's okay." Reluctantly, I loosened my grip on his jersey, preparing to hand it back to him.

But he shook his head. "Keep it" Aiden said firmly. "I don't mind."

"Alright then, see you tomorrow?"

Aiden nodded, tilting his head slightly. "Bye, sweetheart."

The next day

I pushed the huge door of the library, my eyes widening in amazement. The shelves towered above me, filled with books of all shapes and sizes. The sunlight filters through the stained glass windows, creating a beautiful display of colors.

The scent of old books fills the air, and I can't help but feel a sense of curiosity. So this was what they were doing when they were closed.

Wow, the time paid off.

"You're here early" I said, sitting down, facing Aiden. He was comfortably sitting on his chair. I noticed his glasses perched on his face, which meant he's serious. Looks like someone is prepared.

Aiden sighed, "Yeah, we lost a lot of days on this project, so let's catch them up."

I noded. Taking out my things.

"So last time, we couldn't find a template, so let's skip that and start with the project." He instructed

"ok"

—

"No, that's the wrong pattern; we should start by doing this." I groaned, pointing at the screen.

"No, Thompson, that will slow us down." He resorted

"And how are you so sure, huh? We haven't even tried it."

"Because I know"

I took a deep breath and let it out slowly. "You know what? I'm going to be the bigger person. Let's start with your way then."

Aiden grinned. "Let's do it."

A few minutes passed, and to my surprise, his approach seemed to be paying off. Which I hate to admit.

I looked up, catching his gaze. "What?"

He leaned forward, a smile on his face. "You know what, sweetheart."

I rolled my eyes, not wanting to give him satisfaction. "No, I don't"

Please, I was not about to admit to him that he was right. What do I look like? Admitting this to Aiden is like a ticket to constant teasing and never-ending embarrassment. So no.

He chuckled "Well, if you're not going to admit it, I'll just have to rub it in your face. Remember when-"

I cut him off. "You're so childish, Miller. Let's just get back to work."

"Not if you admit that I was right and you were wrong."

I crossed my arms. "Nope"

He got up from his chair, placed his glasses down, and started stretching, letting out a loud groan.

"We've been here for like 15 minutes, not even an hour, so there's no need for that."

He looked down. "I'm an athlete, sweetheart."

"Just come sit down."

"No, let's take a break."

"Break? We've barely progressed, and you want to take a break? Absolutely not."

"So you haven't told me your honest opinion about yesterday" He said, deciding to ignore me.

I raised an eyebrow. "The game? You weren't half bad, I guess" I shrugged

"Not the right answer"

I sighed, giving in, "Okay, you were good." Then instantly cringed. This is something I would have never said to Aiden. But I guess things are different.

He smiled, knowing he had gotten a compliment out of me. "I know"

I rolled my eyes, pushing my things away, knowing that we weren't going to continue any time soon.

Curiosity picked up my mind. "So how long have you been playing football?"

"Aw, I didn't know you cared." Aiden joked while placing his hand on his chest.

"I don't."

He grinned, seeing through my act. "Well, I've been playing since I was a kid. Started with my dad and brother, so about fourteen years."

"You have a brother?"

His demeanour shifted for a second but went back to normal: "Yeah, an older one; he was a real football player, probably better than me."

I noticed that he said; was. Did something happen? Does his brother not play anymore? I decided not to push any further, since it's none of my business.

Shifting the focus away from his family, he turned the conversation towards me.

"What about you?"

"What?"

"You got any siblings."

I shook my head lightly. "Nope, only child."

"That must suck."

Feeling slightly offended by his assumption, I gasped lightly and retorted, "Actually, no, it's not that bad."

He chucked, "That's what they all say."

Rolling my eyes with a small smile "Enough talking about useless things; now let's continue, C'mon." He groaned in response but reluctantly sat down.

—

Wordcount: 1016

18 | Change

I let out a tired sigh, shutting the books one by one. The table was cluttered with a massive stack of books, each one opened to about halfway through.

Feeling the strain in my eyes, I reached up to rub them, glancing at the clock. It read 8:03. Fuck, I thought to myself as I peered outside and noticed that darkness had already settled in. It's that time of year when the days grow shorter and the nights longer.

The library is pretty dark now. There are only a few lamps flickering, giving off a dim lighting. The air feels still and quiet and there was barely anyone; I could only count two.

Standing up and yawning, I noticed Aiden. He was sitting there, completely focused, with a pen in his hand, scribbling away on a piece of paper. His dark brows were furrowed in concentration, and his intense gaze behind those glasses made it hard to look away. It was like he was in his own world, completely absorbed in whatever he was writing.

It was a rare sight, one that left me feeling somewhat intimidated by his presence.

Just as I was lost in my thoughts, my phone rang, pulling me back to reality. I answered with a simple "Hi, mom."

"Do you know what time it is?" She replied coldly, ignoring my greeting.

I sighed "I'm in the library; I'm heading home soon."

There was a brief silence on the other end before she finally said, "Alright, come home soon; be safe"

I replied with a simple "ok" and placed my phone down, rubbing my eyebrows.

"was that your mom?" Aiden asked, I nodded in response. "Yeah, I need to head home."

Aiden took off his glasses, carefully placing them down, and stood up, stretching his body. "Let me walk, you" he offered.

I shook my head, declining his offer. "No, it's alright. My house is just a short fifteen-minute walk away."

"Let me walk you home, Thompson. It's late"

I thought about it for a moment. Than nodded. Even though it's with Aiden, I still didn't want to walk alone, especially since it's this dark outside.

We grabbed our stuff and walked out.

The air was a bit chilly, but a good kind. The leaves were starting to dry since autumn is over and winter is coming soon. My favourite time, by the way, is mainly because it's my birthday season.

I pulled my jacket tighter around me, keen to avoid another cold.

The moon cast a soft glow over the empty streets as we strolled side by side, surrounded by an eerie silence broken only by the gentle rustling of the wind and our own footsteps echoing down the quiet street.

"Do you usually walk late at night by yourself?" Aiden asked, his gaze fixated on me.

"Yes, occasionally when I stay late at school" I replied.

He raised an eyebrow but simply nodded. An awkward silence fell, and I couldn't help but despise the awkwardness that hung in the air. God, I hate awkward silence.

Aiden cleared his throat, breaking the tension. "So, can you believe high school is almost over" he asked.

I rubbed my head. "Yeah, it's hard to wrap my head around it" I admitted.

Aiden nodded. "Have you started thinking about colleges yet? My dad won't stop pressuring me about it."

I paused for a moment, meeting his gaze. "Well, I do have a few in mind, but it still feels too early to make a final decision" I replied. "What about you? Any thoughts on where you want to go?"

"I'm thinking of going to Stanford or Princeton."

Of course he picked the best schools. I remember someone saying that his whole family went to one of those schools, so I guess that's why he chose those.

In that moment, I couldn't help but wonder if his decision was solely based on family tradition or if he genuinely believed those schools were the best fit for him.

"I just can't believe I survived almost four years with you." I sighed, shaking my head.

He chuckled. "Those were the best years of your life; stop denying it. Thompson"

I rolled my eyes.

As we reached my house, we came to a sudden halt. I began walking towards the doorsteps, leaving Aiden standing behind.

"Wait there; I'll be right back" I hurriedly said, darting inside. I passed my father at his desk, making a beeline for my room.

Within seconds, I was back outside. I don't know how a couple flights of stairs could leave me so breathless. I really need to star exercising.

"Here" I said, handing Aiden his jersey. "Thanks for lending it to me the other day, by the way."

A warm smile spread across his face as he gently took the jersey from my hands. "No problem, sweetheart" he replied.

A brief silence settled between us. "Anyways, bye" I said, waving my hands.

He waved back, his smile unwavering. "Good night, Thompson" he called out.

—

I flopped onto my bed, feeling a mix of emotions. Something felt different between Aiden and me. Today, we didn't bicker as much and actually managed to accomplish some work together. Then he walked me home, and we had a conversation that was both awkward and surprisingly normal, without any arguments.

It's not like our usual routine, and I couldn't help but question if I was just imagining things. But deep down, I knew it was real.

Tossing and turning in bed, I let sleep slowly claim me.

wordcount: 929

19 | Ideas

"Under the sea?"

"What is this? spongebob, no."

"How about a Masquerade ball?"

"That's even worse than the first!" I rubbed my eyes.

"Zombie Apocalypse."

"Now you guys are just fucking with me" I groaned.

"Language" Roman warned.

"Hey, come on, guys. Homecoming is just three days away, and we're way off schedule. Can we get back on track?"

I turned towards Roman, noticing his stern expression. "Roman, my friend, please tell me you have something truly amazing to suggest. I need a little spark of inspiration here."

He shrugged, and his gaze met Myvy's. She glanced back at him with a smile. What was that?

"Well, how about we go for something like Hollywood in the 2000s?" she suggested.

I took a moment to consider it. "Good! Thank goodness we have someone here with useful ideas" I exclaimed, shooting a glance at Greyson and Safiya.

The two of them exchanged eye rolls.

Safiya is our media coordinator; she's in charge of managing the council's communication and publicity efforts. Last week, both she and Greyson were sick for some reason; they probably caught my cold, but we never know.

Greyson is our treasurer; he's responsible for managing the financial aspects of the council's activities and events.

"Okay, now that we finally have our theme, let's plan how it will go, then send our ideas to the office." They all nod.

Today was the student council meeting, and we had to choose a theme for homecoming, which is in three days. But thanks to Nora, we're a bit off schedule. She was in charge of getting the necessary papers, but she never did.

And now we have no idea where the hell she is. How fantastic is our vice president?

"Alright, we should now brainstorm some ideas for how the venue should look." Roman said he was checking a box off his notebook.

"It can't be in our budget, though; last time we went past, we remembered what happened." Greyson trailed off, staring at Safiya.

"Yeah, I wonder who's fault that was" Safiya mumbled loud enough for us to hear.

Greyson shot her a look, then opened his mouth, about to say something.

"Guys. It's time to be serious." I interrupted, standing up. "We only have two days to prepare this thing; it's either we finish it all today or no one leaves; remember, I have the keys." I said, juggling the key around my finger.

—

As time went on, we all got caught up in our own tasks but still managed to help each other. Myvy and Roman seemed particularly close, and I couldn't help but wonder if there was more going on between them.

Although I've always thought of Roman as someone who isn't interested in relationships, but hey, you never know what can happen.

As the sun began to set, my phone started ringing. Aiden? I paused, squinting to see the name closer. Did he actually put a red heart emoji next to his name? This guy cannot be real.

Deciding to ignore his call, I started packing things up. It was time to wrap things up for the day.

Safiya was the first one to leave, as she bid her goodbyes and left swiftly, followed by Greyson.

Roman scoffed, "Those two, first to leave and last to arrive"

"They probably have other things to take care of after school, Roman" Myvy replied. She gently placed her hand on his shoulder and then turned to me, handing over a paper. "Here are all the ideas we came up with. I wrote them down for you to submit to the office."

I nod. "Thanks a lot, Myvy."

A few minutes later, both Myvy and Roman departed, leaving me to lock the door with my key.

"Good evening, Zhera." A soft, croaky voice startled me.

"Oh, Mr. Benson! Good evening. Are you back from your break already?" I asked, surprised.

He nodded, closing his eyes. "Yes, I spent some time with my kids in Thailand."

"That's wonderful." I replied, leaning from one leg to another.

"I know you're in a hurry, but before you go, here." Mr. Benson reached into his pockets and pulled out a small souvenir.

"My granddaughter gave it to me. She told me to give it to someone it reminded me of, and you came to mind." He handed the souvenir to me.

A soft smile graced my lips as I held the pendant in front of me. It was a beautiful violet flower.

"Thank you so much, sir" I said gratefully.

Mr. Bennett hummed a light tone as he made his way past me, his hands crossed behind him.

Mr. Bennett is the school's janitor; he's the oldest worker in the school. I've known him since I stepped into this school; he's like a granddad to me.

—

Meet me in English class - Aiden

20 | Contact

I left him on scene while rolling my eyes. Now why did this dumbass decide to do it in a classroom? Don't we usually work at the library?

As I entered the classroom, I noticed Aiden sitting in his usual seat, engrossed in his phone. He looked up and waved at me.

As I took my seat, facing him, I noticed that Aiden was still watching me, a smirk playing on his lips. I felt a twinge of annoyance, but I tried to brush it off.

"What is it?"

He glanced at my phone. "You like my name?"

"Oh yeah, I almost forgot. When the hell did you even change it?"

He laughed. "That's a secret, Thompson."

"creep." I muttered under my breath while placing my bag beside me.

I started glancing around while fanning myself: "Is it hot in here or Is it just me?"

"It's you." Aiden quickly replied.

I got up from my seat and tried to open the huge windows. The hell? Is this thing stuck? I pushed again harder, but it still wouldn't budge.

Am I this weak? I mean, I knew I wasn't the most physically strong, but I'm completely weak. I huffed, tilting my head down.

I suddenly felt a presence behind me, and in a swift motion, the windows opened widely. I grunted, and of course Aiden opened it with a flick of his wrist.

I turned around and saw him gaze down at me, the corners of his lips forming up. "That's how you do it, sweetheart."

Lightly pushing him away, I made my way back to my seat. "I was about to do it, you know."

He scoffed, sitting back down. "Yeah, you struggling and out of breath is you about to do it."

"Whatever, let's just finish our project"

30 minutes later

The room was quiet. The sun had almost finished setting. As the sun's rays pierced through the window, its golden hues cast a glow in the classroom, which was hitting me directly in the face. I couldn't help but squint my eyes in discomfort.

Despite my attempts to shield myself, the golden light continued to illuminate.

Suddenly, I caught Aiden's gaze, and he flashed a smile in my direction. His eyes held a soft look. Maybe even admiration?

I raised my eyebrow.

"Too much sun?"

"mhm"

He got up from his seat, making his way towards mine. "Let's switch; I don't mind the sun."

I nodded and got up.

When I gazed up, the sunlight embraced him, illuminating his eyes with a radiant glow. The dark hazel shade transformed into a lighter, more captivating hue. The sun's touch highlighted his lips, giving them a soft, pinkish tint. He looked absolutely mesmerizing. That's the word that came to mind: mesmerizing.

I cleared my throat, catching his attention. "I forgot to ask, why are we here? and not in the library."

"The library was packed. I know how you don't like to work with too many people around you."

He's right; most of the time, I like working by myself or when there aren't a lot of people around. But since when did he know that?

I simply nodded, refocusing on the project. As I dove into my work, a wave of frustration washed over me. I found myself biting at my pencil, realizing that I had hit a block, furrowing my brows in confusion.

This research does not make sense; the words do not correlate with the facts. Wait, think Zhera think. I found myself biting harder on my pencil now.

Should I ask Aiden? I mean, I'm struggling with something, so it's only right to ask my partner about it. This is our project, after all. Setting aside my ego and dignity, I mustered up the courage to ask him for help.

"Miller" I whispered, my voice barely audible.

He glanced up. "hm?"

I let out a sigh. "I need your help."

Aiden couldn't resist a smirk, crossing his arms around his chest. "Sorry, I couldn't quite catch that. Mind repeating it for me?"

"You heard me"

He shook his head with a mischievous twinkle in his eyes. "Nope, I don't think I did"

Inhaling sharply, I maintained eye contact, not ready to play along. "I said, I need your help with something."

"What's the magic word, sweetheart?"

"Miller."

"Thompson."

This repulsive vixen, I could feel frustration building within me as Aiden continued to tease. It took a lot of courage for me to ask for his help, and his response was not what I had hoped for.

"Please" I whispered, my head down.

Aiden leaned in closer, a mischievous smile on his face. "Huh? Repeat that."

"Please, Miller," I said a bit louder this time, trying to maintain my composure.

He chuckled, seemingly satisfied. "Now, that wasn't so hard, was it?"

My frustration got the better of me, and I snapped, "Fuck you."

Aiden raised an eyebrow. "You would?"

I was taken aback by his response. What did he mean by that?

In a swift moment, he was crouching beside me while laughing at his joke. "At your service, Thompson."

I rolled my eyes "I need help with this; I don't understand what it means; the research doesn't make sense."

He hums, analyzing it. I turned my face around to face him; his jaw was clenched and his brows furrowed. His face then shifted.

He turned to face me; our faces were now mere inches apart, and we both became aware of the sudden I quickly turned away, clearing my throat, and he did the same. "So?" I asked

"You'll just have to switch this up and find another site."

I nod, "Thanks."

He grins. "You see, there's no harm in asking for help."

"Where is she?" I heard Ciara's voice and her footsteps echoing through the halls.

" I think she's in English class. Zhera, are you there?" Kehlani's voice followed. Their conversation came to an abrupt halt as they spotted Aiden and me inches away from each other.

Aiden stood up, breaking the silence. "Hi, ladies."

They both waved awkwardly. I quickly stood up, attempting to diffuse the awkwardness. "Hey, guys, Just give me a moment; I'll be done soon. Meet me in front."

"Kk!" they exclaimed while rushing off.

I turned around to face Aiden. "I guess I have to go now."

"Yeah, see you. Thompson."

—

wordcount: 1065

21 | Question

"**T**hese dresses are so expensive," I said as I checked the price tags of the dresses. "Don't worry, my dad's got it covered," Ciara reassured me, flashing a black card.

"Are you sure?"

"Yeah, he said, since this is our last homecoming, he's going to spoil us."

"That's why I love your dad, Ciara," Kehlani chimed in as she emerged from the changing room.

"A little too much, if you ask me," I muttered under my breath.

"So, how does this dress look?" Kehlani twirled around in a beautiful beige gown with a long, open back. Ciara and I both squealed, "Oh my gosh, it looks so good on you. I told you you should've tried a new colour."

"Yeah, green definitely isn't my color."

We're currently dress shopping for homecoming tomorrow. At this high-end boutique that was clearly not my usual scene, you should see the prices way above my budget.

A tall and elegant blonde woman approached us with a warm smile. "You ladies, alright?" she inquired with a friendly smile.

I glanced at Ciara, who gave me a knowing look. "Actually, my friend here is having a bit of a hard time finding something she really likes," Ciara chimed in, her eyes scanning the racks of expensive dresses.

Her offer put me at ease, and I mustered a smile. "I'm looking for something elegant yet comfortable."

She took a moment to carefully examine the dresses around the shop, her eyes scanning the racks. Then, with a stride, she began to make her way to the other side of the boutique. I followed behind reluctantly.

"Well, we do have a few options that might fit your criteria. Let me show you a couple of dresses that could be just what you're looking for."

I nodded, getting closer. She looked me up and down. "You're a bit on the taller side; I'm guessing you'll want a longer dress."

"yup."

"Alright then, what colour do you lean towards?" she asked.

"I'm more into lighter colours, like light blue, purple, or even black," I replied.

She nodded and shifted through a rack of clothes, pulling out three dresses. "Try these on in the fitting rooms over there, and we'll see how they look."

I thanked her and headed towards the changing rooms.

The first dress I tried on was a light pink one. It had a cute design, but the front was very revealing and made me feel like my breasts could slip out at any moment. Needless to say, it wasn't the right choice for me. I decided not to show it to Khelani and Ciara since I wasn't a fan of it myself.

The second dress, on the other hand, was absolutely beautiful. It was a black off-the-shoulder dress with an open back that was tied with delicate strings. It didn't make me too uncomfortable and had a pretty long slit on the sides. I felt much more confident in this one.

I stepped out of the changing room. "So?"

Their faces lit up with surprise and awe. Kehlani was the first to say, "You look so hot!"

Ciara nodded enthusiastically, a huge smile on her face. "I never thought I'd see you in a dress like this, Zhera."

I couldn't help but blush at their compliments. "Aw, stop, you guys."

The lady assisting us chimed in with a soft smile, "It looks like we found the one. I don't think you need to try on the last dress."

"Yeah, I agree."

—

"Guys, I'm so excited!" Kehlani squealed, taking a delectable bite of Ciara's mom's homemade cookies.

"Keh, you really shouldn't be eating while wearing the face mask. Let it dry properly." Ciara said as she positioned my face.

"But your mom's cookies are the best, Ciara," she moaned while closing her eyes.

I shook my head with a smile. While Ciara brusquely tilted it back up

"Do we even need these face masks? We look like aliens." I remarked, checking myself in the small mirror.

"Stop moving, and yes, we do. I finally found a mask that can be used on all three of our faces without any consequences." She paused, casting a glance towards Kehlani, which made her instantly stop eating. "So trust me when I say we'll look amazing tomorrow."

Kehlani positioned herself on the kitchen counter, trying to discreetly take another chunk of cookies.

"Who are you guys taking as your dates?"

I scratched my head while shrugging. Me and guys don't go together. Yes, I've had my fair share of crushes and all, but no serious relationships. I guess I've always liked to prioritize my studies and not some high school boy and relationships.

Some people would say I've missed out on the high school "love experience", but it honestly doesn't bother me. I would take education over boys any day.

Khelani blushed. "I'm going with Alejandro."

Ciara and I exchanged glances, unable to contain our smiles. It seemed that our long-awaited ship had finally set sail. What should their ship name be, Kehlandro?

"When did he ask you out?"

A grin spread across Khelani's face as she confidently replied, "Actually, I was the one who asked him."

I was a bit taken aback but not surprised; it's Kehlani after all. "Not surprising, Khe, your confidence is off the roof."

Ciara nodded. "Yeah, not every girl has the guts to make the first move like you did."

Khelani's smile widened; she looked very proud.

I looked up at Ciara, her brow furrowed in concentration. "I'm guessing you're going with Michael, right?"

"Yeah, he texted me."

Texted? Don't you usually ask someone out in person? Am I the only one who finds this a bit odd?

"Alright, all done. Your skin is about to look amazing tomorrow." She chirped while clapping her hands.

I went to sit beside Kehlani on the counter. I tried to take the cookie but she swiftly swatted my hand away. I gave her a pointed look, while furrowing my eyebrows.

"You guys are incredible; can't you go ten minutes without devouring a cookie?"

"It's not just any cookie, C; it's your mom's."

She shook her head, approaching us and leaning on the counter. "So, Zhera, we still need to talk about you and Aiden."

"What? There's nothing between me and Aiden."

Aiden and I shouldn't even be mentioned in the same sentence, let alone imply that something might be going on. I'd rather die.

"Then explain what happened the other day. Why was he so close to you?"

"Yeah, you guys looked like you were about to lock lips." Khelani said.

I rolled my eyes. "He was just helping me with a question, nothing more, nothing less."

"It didn't seem like nothing."

"Don't-."

"What's this I'm hearing about a boy?" Ciara's dad came downstairs, inter-rupting me. He had a tight black tank top and loose jogging pants.

"Hi, mister Daniel." Kehlani greeted him with a huge smile plastered on her face.

"Hello, ladies. I hope I'm not overhearing any talk about boys." Mr. Daniel inquired, raising an eyebrow skeptically, as he made his way towards the cupboard.

"No, Daddy, it's nothing important," Ciara responded quickly.

Mr. Daniel's expression remained unconvinced: "It didn't sound like 'nothing' to me."

Just then, Ciara's mother emerged from the living room. "Oh, come on, Daniel. They're teenagers; that's what they do. Remember us in high school?" She paused for a second, her expression changing. "We were way worse."

"No, we don't want to remember you guys in high school, mom." Ciara groaned disgustingly.

Mr. Daniel seemed hesitant but eventually relented. "But they're still just kids. No boyfriends until you're married, alright?"

We all awkwardly nodded. While both he and Ciara's mom went upstairs in fits of giggles, About to reminisce their high school years.

I couldn't help but ponder Ciara's words. Is there actually something going on between Aiden and me? ugh, that just sounds strange and just plain out wrong. I've known him for almost four years now and have never felt anything but pure dislike. So what's this talk about there being something between us?

Is there really something between us?

—

wordcount: 1384 ohh, looks like Zhera's starting to question her relationship with Aiden. We'll find out more in the next chapter;)

22 | Homecoming

"Guys, I have to leave soon." I mentioned while hastily brushing my hair.

"Aw, I wanted all three of us to go together," Kehlani expressed, approaching me and gently pulling the hairbrush from my grasp. "Please be gentle, or your hair will end up messy."

I smiled. "Thanks; I'm just feeling a bit stressed cause I want to make sure everything is perfect before the dance starts."

"Don't worry, I have complete faith that it will turn out perfect," Ciara reassured me as she focused on applying her makeup at her vanity table.

I checked the time. Homecoming starts at 6:30, but I had to be there forty minutes earlier so that I could ensure everything was perfect.

"By the way, who came up with the theme idea? It's so pretty." Khelani asked, humming to the song playing.

Lana Del Rey | Diet Mountain Dew

"It was Myvy."

She seemed surprised. "The shy girl?"

"Tell her that the theme is amazing, way better than last year's." Ciara, who was adorning her hair with small crystal gems, said.

"I don't even remember what last year's theme was."

"That's because you didn't attend it, Zhera."

"oh yeah.." I trailed off. Last year, I didn't attend because my mom didn't let me. She found out that I had a pretty low grade on my english quiz, so she grounded me and forbade me from attending the dance. Mind you, the quiz didn't even count towards our final grades.

I like my mom and all, but she can be a bit too much. But she's just looking out for me, right?

"I love Mrs. Thompson and all, but sometimes I wouldn't know how to deal with her; I don't know how you do it, Zehra." Kehlani admitted

I sighed. "I know she's just looking out for me, but sometimes she can be a bit too harsh. I love her, but dealing with her can be impossible."

I don't even know how I do it.

Just then, Ciara's mom entered the room with a tray of freshly baked cookies, her eyes twinkling with delight. "Hello, girls! Would you like some cookies? They're still warm from the oven," she explained.

"Don't mind if I do!" Khelani eagerly rushed to grab the cookies from her hands, thanking her.

"Guys, I have no idea what to do with my hair." I sighed, my brows furrowed, as I gazed at my reflection in the vanity mirror.

Being in a rush gave me zero time too think about what I should do with my hair.

Ciara's mom approached me with a gentle smile. "You want some help, honey?" she asked while wiping her hands on her apron.

"Yes please."

"Come, here, beautiful." She motioned for me to approach with a gentle smile, then began to carefully style my hair, using her hands to tame the unruly locks into a beautiful, sleek finish. The soothing touch of her hands and the warmth of the cookies filled the room, creating a cozy and comforting atmosphere.

Just what I needed before going. She swiftly finished, and I turned towards the mirror to admire myself. My hair was styled in a cute half-up, half-down ponytail with a slick side part that added an elegant touch. The only thing left to do was to curl the ends.

"What do you think, Hunny?"

I admired it. "It's absolutely beautiful; thank you."

"Ohh, Zehra's hair looks amazing; can you do a similar style for me, Miss?" Kehlani asked, her voice tinged with longing as she took a final bite of her cookie.

"Me too, mommy?" Ciara pleaded with puppy eyes.

She chuckled warmly and nodded, her eyes crinkling at the corners. "Alright, come here, you two," she beckoned, her voice gentle.

—

After the millions of pictures we took, I arrived at school in less than twenty minutes. It was currently 6:00, so I made it right on time. After finishing my hair and makeup and also taking almost ten minutes to put on my dress, I was finally done.

I began to make my way inside, my expression quickly shifting.

The entrance was decorated with a red carpet, just like at movie premieres, that would lead students into the main hall. Large posters featuring famous movie stars were hung on the walls, creating an immersive atmosphere.

The hallways were transformed into walkways that looked like famous Hollywood streets. Large banners with iconic Hollywood landmarks, like the Hollywood sign or the Walk of Fame stars, were hung along the walls.

The school truly outdid itself this time. There were already people here, and they all greeted me when I passed by.

One girl in particular caught my attention, her eyes scanning me from head to toe before exclaiming, "Oh my goodness, you look absolutely stunning!"

Her compliment brought a smile to my face, and I graciously thanked her. Then continued to make my way towards the main hall, my excitement growing with each step.

My eyes widened as I stepped inside.

It was transformed into a glamorous ballroom reminiscent of a movie set. The ceiling is adorned with twinkling lights to create a starry night effect. Tables were covered with black and gold tablecloths, and centrepieces featured miniature Oscar statues. Balloons in gold, silver, and black colours can be seen scattered around the room to add an extra touch of elegance.

I cannot believe this is the final product. It is way beyond my imagination. I do hope that we didn't go over the budget. Otherwise, we're screwed.

"Zhera, over here." Greyson's voice resonated across the room. I turned my head and spotted him standing alongside Myvy and Roman. I made my way towards them, admiring the stunning transformation of the venue.

"We really outdid ourselves, guys. The place looks absolutely amazing."

Roman looked around, a slight smile playing on his lips. "We truly did," He was dressed in a dark blue tuxedo with a black tie. Simple but nice

"By the way, you look wonderful, President." Myvy murmured softly, her cheeks tinged with a blush.

"Thank you. You look beautiful as well." Myvy's delicate pink dress caught my attention; it featured a subtle slit on the side, adding a touch of allure to her appearance.

I sighed; everything was perfect.

Perfectly perfect

—

word count: 1051

23 | Strange

6:40

Homecoming finally started, and everything was not perfectly fine. Don't get me wrong, the place still looked amazing. All the students had beautiful gowns and suits, each different colour; they really embodied the theme, but other than that, nothing was going right.

As the students started to pile up, we realized there were way too many, that we attended. We usually give out tickets that the students have to purchase early. They are free, of course, but we had that system to make sure they didn't pile up.

"Zhera, what should we do?" Safiya asked, concern written all over her face.

Taking a minute to collect myself, I replied, "First, let's calm down; there's obviously nothing we can do right now. To manage this in the future, we could implement a stricter ticketing system. This way, the students would need to secure their tickets in advance." I paused for a second, catching my breath. "Is that alright?"

Everyone reluctantly nodded. "Alright, now let's get back to what we were doing previously."

As we made our way back, I couldn't help but notice the sight of Myvy and Roman walking together. Interesting

6:50

"Zhera, are you finally finished with your meeting? Come on, let's hit the dance floor," Kehlani exclaimed, pulling me towards the lively rhythm. I chuckled as I followed along.

"Where's Ciara?" My eyes scanned the room, searching for her familiar face. "Oh, she's waiting at the entrance for her date."

"He's still not here?" I remarked, a hint of surprise in my voice. It had already been thirty minutes since the dance began, and he's still not he re..strange.

"Where's your date?" I shouted over the booming music. The crowded dance floor was starting to make me feel a bit uncomfortable.

"Oh, he'll be coming later. He had football practice," Kehlani explained amidst the loud beats.

Before I could reply, I felt a hand wrap around mine. "Zhera, we have a problem."

7:01

"The DJ is pissed off at Mason and Liam because they kept on throwing pranks." Sebastian explained with a frown.

I couldn't help but let out a sigh, shifting my gaze towards the direction where the mischievous duo was seated. Roman, in an attempt to diffuse the situation, was delivering a stern lecture to the twins, while Myvy was trying to calm down the agitated DJ.

Mason and Liam are the infamous Alderidges, a very rich family. Which is one of the main reasons why I think they scored a spot in the academy.

I mean, seriously, how else could they have made it in? They're not exactly the brightest bulbs, and they're always up to some pointless prank.

It's just so frustrating how the wealthy seem to slide by without any consequences. I made my way toward them. "Roman, could you guys please give us a moment?" I said it with a sweet smile. He nodded and escorted the DJ out of the room. Myvy is closely following behind.

As soon as they left, my sweet smile faded away, replaced by a more serious expression. "So I've heard you two have been pulling some pranks around here?"

They exchanged glances before chuckling, seemingly finding amusement in the situation.

I tilted my head to the side. "What's so funny?"

Mason couldn't help but snort before responding, "Oh, nothing, president."

"Go on." Liam finished

"No, I want to know what's so funny."

The twins glanced at each other for a second. One of them raised an eyebrow and casually scratched their head before responding. "We never knew that our president was this hot." He remarked, his words laced with a hint of amusement.

My face scrunched up in disgust. "What a very weird way to compliment someone."

"You asked us for an answer, and we delivered."

I stayed silent for a second, arms crossed. "So if I tell you guys something, would you deliver?"

The pair looked at each other before saying, "Depends."

7:10

I emerged from the room, a smile playing on my lips, while the twins trailed behind me, their heads bowed low.

Roman raised an eyebrow. "What happened in there?"

Sebastian chimed in, noting the unusual demeanour of the twins: "They don't seem like their usual selves."

"I just told them something—nothing to worry about. Now I'm going to go talk to the DJ and try to reason with him. Everything's all good."

I turned around to leave before noticing Myvy staring at me with a look on her face. I smirked back with a shrug.

—

After having a chat with the DJ, I finally convinced him to stay, reminding him of how much he gets paid for being here.

I then decided to take a moment for myself and stepped out onto a small balcony. The atmosphere outside was invigorating, with a fresh breeze that carried a slight chill but was nonetheless pleasant.

With my eyes closed, I allowed myself to exhale deeply, releasing a breath that had been unknowingly held within me.

A crease formed on my forehead as I sensed the presence of someone else joining me on the balcony. Despite this realization, I chose not to open my eyes; I was too lazy to do so.

"Thompson?"

I turned around when I heard that familiar voice. There stood Aiden, a look of surprise evident on his face. My eyes travelled down. He wore a tailored suit that accentuated his lean physique. The midnight blue fabric brought out the colour of his eyes, making them appear even more captivating. The suit was perfectly fitted, emphasizing his whole body.

His dark hair was pulled back nicely, revealing his sharp features and chiselled jawline. His piercing eyes were a captivating shade of hazel that were eliminated by the moonlight, framed by thick, well-groomed eyebrows.

Aiden looked a bit different today. I don't know how exactly, but he looked different.

"oh, hi." I stumbled in my response. As he drew nearer, his gaze delicately traced the contours of my face. "You look beautiful," he whispered softly.

A faint smile graced my lips, and a rush of warmth surged through me, causing a blush on my cheeks. I really do not know how to take compliments.

This felt weird. I felt weird. Aiden of all people giving me a compliment felt weird; the compliment was simple yet it held an impact on me. It felt strange coming from him, out of everyone who complimented me today; his carried a certain weight that set it apart from the others.

The atmosphere around us seemed to shift, a subtle tension building as we exchanged glances. Aiden's gaze was intense, his focus momentarily lost in the vast expanse of the sky.

And as I returned his gaze, I couldn't help but wonder what thoughts were running through his mind, accompanied by that gentle smile he held.

"The sky is beautiful, isn't it?" Aiden asked, while admiring the sky, his features were enhanced by the moonlight. Hazel eyes, deep and mesmerizing, reflected the stars above.

I stared at him while nodding, "Yeah, it's beautiful."

"I didn't think you would come," he said, breaking the silence that had settled between us.

I rubbed my arms, trying to ward off the slight chill in the air. "Yeah, I decided to," I replied softly. "After all, this is our last one."

"It is."

A comfortable silence enveloped us, interrupted only by the distant chirping of crickets and the faint strains of music playing in the background.It felt nice to be away from the loud music and just everything else. Tonight had been a disappointment in many ways.

Finally, some peace and quiet.

—

wordcount: 1281

24 | Night

My peace and quiet were cut short when

"Zhera-" Khelani abruptly interrupted, but her words trailed off as she caught sight of Aiden and me standing together. Her eyes widened with surprise.

Khelani's eyes darted between us. She clearly hadn't expected to find us here.

"Hey, Aiden," she greeted. He simply waved back.

"What is it?"

Without a response, Khelani urged me to follow her, her grip on my hand firm and insistent.

As we walked away, Khelani's words tumbled out in a rush, her voice laced with anxiety. "It's an emergency; come," she urged, grasping my hand in hers.

I looked back at Aiden for a second, then followed her.

—

"Wait, wait, what's going on? I was in the middle of-" began to say, but before I could finish, Kehlani interrupted. "What? Having a moment with your boyfriend?"

I stopped in my tracks "Kehlani." She quickly apologized, noticing the look on my face, and guided me outside, this time with a gentler touch.

"It's Ciara; she's not doing well," she explained. My heart sank at the mention of Ciara's name. "Is it because of Michael?" I blurted out, my worry intensifying.

"yes."

We approached Ciara, finding her sitting on a bench with her head hanging low. "C, what's wrong?" I asked, taking a seat beside her.

She glanced at me briefly and shook her head. "I'm guessing Kehlani already filled you in. He's not coming. I've been waiting for over an hour now, and he hasn't even bothered to text me back," she whispered, her voice barely audible.

I've never trusted that boy since the very first moment I laid eyes on him. My suspicions have only grown stronger over time.

I nodded understandingly, realizing that Ciara wasn't in the mood to talk at the moment.

Kehlani sat beside her, offering comfort by gently massaging her back. We sat in silence until Ciara broke it.

"This isn't the first time he's done this," she paused for a moment, then sighed, "Forget it, I'm just going to go home."

I quickly stood up. "Come on, Ce," I urged, hoping to change her mind.

"Don't let a boy ruin your entire night," Kehlani added, her face scowling in disapproval. Ciara shook her head. "No, I want to go. The night is already ruined."

I stayed quiet, knowing that there was not the point of stopping her. "I'll use my car to get home." Ciara stood up while checking her phone. "You guys have your rides, right?"

Kehlani and I reluctantly nodded.

—

"I feel bad for C" Khelani expressed, her voice tinged with disappointment. "I actually thought he was a good guy." She paused, noticing my hesitation to follow her back inside. "What's wrong?"

"I think I'll head home. I just need to sit down for a bit before I leave." I replied, my voice filled with a mix of exhaustion and longing,

She looked back at me. "Are you sure?"

I nodded, trying to reassure her, "Yeah, go spend some time with Alejandro. I know you've been wanting to see him."

With a warm hug, she made her way back inside, leaving me to my thoughts.

As I sat on the bench, exhausted and disappointed by how the day had turned out, I couldn't help but feel a sense of relief as my body sank into the wooden seat.

The event that was supposed to be fun and unforgettable had instead left me drained and my toes aching from all the walking. The night was descending, bringing with it a chill that seemed to seep into my bones.

Lost in my thoughts, I was startled when the sound of the door opening broke through the silence. I turned my head to see Aiden stepping outside.

His expression was one of confusion, as if he were searching for someone. Our eyes met, and a smile slowly spread across his face. With purposeful strides, he made his way towards me.

"Hi, sweetheart."

"Why are you here? Didn't you just arrive?"

He shrugged while taking a seat beside her. "These things aren't really my thing."

"You didn't go to last year's one?"

"Nope, I didn't feel like it. Especially since someone wasn't coming."

Someone? Was it his date? That would've been hilarious. I never really took Aiden for someone who wouldn't be interested in things like this. But then again, it's Aiden.

Aiden leaned forward, his legs spread slightly, and our legs touched as he turned towards me with a smile.

"What?"

His smile widened. "It feels like it's been ages since I last saw you."

I raised an eyebrow. "Didn't we just see each other like three days ago?"

"Yeah, it feels like a long time." He leaned back. "You know, I kind of missed you."

"you did?"

A smile played on his lips as he responded, "Yeah, I missed your annoying self that always thinks that you're right and the arguments you start."

I chuckled, rolling my eyes. "You're not funny." When I turned to face him, I noticed a look of surprise on his face. "What's wrong?"

He seemed taken aback as he replied, "I just never thought I would see you smile, let alone laugh."

My smile faded. "Come on, don't make it sound like I'm some joyless troll."

We've known each other for years. This can't be the first time he's seen me laugh. He quickly raised his arms defensively. "Hey, those were your words, not mine."

With a soft smile, I shook my head and stood up, gently massaging my hands. "I think I'm going to head home now." The night had taken an unexpectedly pleasant turn, all thanks to Aiden. This conversation felt different from our previous ones. It was genuine, without any arguments.

Aiden stood up beside me, his expression briefly shifting before returning to normal. "Do you have a ride?"

I shook my head, a hint of gratitude in my voice. "Nope, I'm just going to Uber."

I came here with one of Ciara's drivers, but I don't want to bother her, so I'll just call an Uber.

"No, let me drive you."

I raised an eyebrow, surprised. "Are you sure?"

"Mhm."

—

As the car pulled into my neighbourhood, I began gathering my things.

"Here we are," Aiden said. I opened the car door, ready to step outside. "Thanks for the ride."

But before I could leave, Aiden gently held my hands, stopping me in my tracks. "Wait, you've got something," he said, brushing a stray strand of hair behind my ear.

I instinctively touched the spot he had fixed. "Aiden-"

He smiled warmly. "You had a piece of hair sticking out. See you on Monday, okay? Our usual spot."

I nodded softly. "Mhm. Goodnight."

"Goodnight, sweetheart,"

—

wordcount: 1138

this chapter was kinda cute wasn't it? I was smiling the whole time while writting it

25 | Thoughts

Tonight was different. Thoughts of Aiden Miller kept flooding my mind. This is something that usually happens, but these thoughts are different. Before, they were thinking about how annoying he was, but it's different.

I actually had a good night today thanks to him. As soon as he came, the atmosphere shifted and I felt nice. Tonight was nice.

I've never felt like this since I was with him. Something feels different, and I've been feeling it this whole night while I was with him.

Since being in his company, I haven't experienced these emotions to such a degree before. There's an obvious shift in the air, and throughout the entire night spent with him, this feeling has been ever-present.

It's as if something different had transpired, and I can't help but revel in it.

Don't tell me.

The next day

"Oh, my head hurts." I groaned as I made my way downstairs.

"You better not have been drinking yesterday, Zhera," my mom warned, with a skeptical look as she sipped her coffee.

"Don't worry, mom, I wasn't." I could see the doubt lingering in her eyes as she raised both eyebrows, clearly unconvinced.

Rolling my eyes in response, I continued on my way to the refrigerator to find something to ease my headache.

My dad chimed in from behind me as he made his way downstairs. "Let her live, Hunny; she's almost eighteen, you know," he interjected.

"Keyword: almost, which is not eighteen," she emphasized.

"Mom, I'm turning eighteen in like a couple of weeks."

"Ah, Zhera, you're all grown up now." My father cooed with a warm smile.

My birthday was just around the corner, in mid-December, and I'm both excited and not about it. It feels like just another day that will pass by.

The only good thing about it is that it's around the time we go on our senior winter trip. So I'm excited about that.

Spending my birthday with my friends in the city of New York seems like something straight out of a movie. Oh yeah, I forgot to mention we're going to New York for our trip.

My dad's words brought me back to the present, and I smiled softly. "I know, Dad," I replied, with a sigh.

"So who dropped you off last night? that was a nice car"

I came to a sudden halt, unsure of how to respond. "Uh, it was Aiden," I replied, my voice slightly faltering.

"Oh, so you guys are friends now?" my mom inquired, curiosity lacing her words.

"Not exactly," I replied, my tone tinged with uncertainty.

The truth was, I couldn't quite classify what Aiden and I were to each other. We weren't complete strangers, but at the same time, we weren't exactly friends either. Our conversations were a mix of constant bickering and occasional normal conversations. However, lately, things have been different, and I found it hard to put into words.

I sighed, realizing that our relationship was difficult to explain.

As I continued doing my breakfast, I felt my dad's stare on me. I looked back and spotted him smiling—the same look he had when Aiden was at my house.

—

I couldn't help but groan as I walked into first period. It was my so-called "favourite" class, but that was before I realized I had to endure the presence of none other than Michael.

As I made my way to my seat, I couldn't help but notice Michael had already settled in his spot, surrounded by not one, not two, but three girls. I couldn't believe the nerve of that guy, letting girls fawn over him like that after what happened.

I couldn't help but overhear one of the girls say, "Michael, your hair looks absolutely amazing today. Can I, like, touch it?"

Michael just casually nodded and said, "Go ahead."

Ugh, the audacity! It was like they were under some kind of spell or something. I couldn't help but scoff at the whole interaction.

"Michael, what do you think of the school so far?" a girl sitting on his desk asked.

"It's not bad; it's filled with nice people and beautiful girls."

They all chuckled.

Someone put a gun to my head, please.

"Hey everyone, let's get settled in," the teacher said as he entered the classroom.

"Thanks," I muttered under my breath, relieved that the girls finally returned to their seats and Michael adjusted himself.

I could feel his gaze on me as he turned to face me. "Good morning, Zhera," he greeted, trying to be all nice and friendly. Bitch

I simply nodded curtly, making it clear that I wasn't interested in engaging with him. I didn't even bother to give him a glance.

—

Soon as the bell rang, I wasted no time making my way out of the classroom.

But before I could get too far, I heard Michael's voice calling out from behind me. He reached out and grabbed my hands, trying to stop me in my tracks. I quickly pulled away, not wanting to be touched by people who were obviously not close to me.

"What do you want?" I asked, slightly annoyed.

"Have you thought about what I asked you last time?" he inquired, sounding hopeful.

I raised an eyebrow, pretending to be oblivious. "And what was that, exactly?"

"You know about tutoring me," he reminded me.

I couldn't help but scoff at his request. "Sorry, but I'm way too busy for that. So if you'll excuse me," I trailed off, starting to walk away.

"Well, at least think about it!" he shouted after me.

I couldn't help but roll my eyes. "Yeah, sure," I muttered sarcastically, not really intending to give it any serious consideration.

This guy has to be crazy if he thinks I'm actually going to tutor him.

When I finally reached my locker, a sense of relief washed over me. I quickly went to check myself in the mirror, making sure my hair and makeup were on point. But just as I started adjusting my uniform, someone interrupted my little routine.

"Hi, Zhera!" Kehlani sang, her voice filled with excitement as she enveloped me in a tight hug.

I couldn't help but chuckle at her energy. "Someone's in a good mood this morning," I teased playfully.

She lowered her head with a blush. "Yeah, yesterday was amazing for me. After you guys left, I spent the whole night with Alejandro. It was incredible. And, um, we also kissed," she whispered in the last part, her head slightly lowered.

My eyes widened. "Aww, Khe, I'm so happy for you!" I exclaimed, unable to contain my joy. I immediately went in for a tight hug, wanting to celebrate this special moment with her.

"Where's Ciara?" I asked eagerly. "We have to celebrate this amazing moment!"

"She's not coming; I texted her this morning, and she said she wasn't in the mood to come."

"oh"

Ciara isn't usually the type to stay at home after something happens. I guess this whole Michael thing got the best of her. or did something else also happen?

I groaned, "Fuck, I think this Michael thing got the best of her."

Kehlani nodded in agreement, her eyes widening as she glanced behind me. A sense of déjà vu washed over me; something like this had already happened.

"Your boy toy's here," she teased, a smirk playing on her lips.

Curiosity piqued, and I turned around to see Aiden down the hallway. Our eyes met, and he wasted no time in making his way towards me. My heart skipped a beat as I watched him approach.

I turned back to face Kehlani, but she was already walking away, mouthing something that I couldn't quite catch. I shrugged it off, knowing that Kehlani always had a flair for the dramatic.

"Good morning, sweetheart." Aiden greeted me with a warm smile.

"Morning," I replied, feeling a bit shy all of a sudden.

He smiled, his eyes filled with genuine interest. "you heading to class now?"

"Yeah,"

"Let me walk you there," Aiden offered, his voice gentle. We began walking side by side, navigating the hallways together. In that moment, it felt as though we were the only two people in the world, the silence broken only by the soft rhythm of my racing heart.

—wordcount: 1377

26 | Internal

"Alright, class, today we will be talking about college applications and scholarships. I know you guys have a couple of months left, but the school likes to be in advance."

I leaned back in my chair, my mind swirling with thoughts about life after high school. The pressure to make the right decision weighed heavily on me, knowing that this was my final year.

Law has always intrigued me, specifically criminal law. On the other hand, there was medicine, a field my mom had always dreamed I would pursue. I did find it interesting, but it didn't make me feel as good as the law did.

Law was something that I was always interested in. I get to explore the intricacies of the legal system, learn about different areas of law, and develop multiple skills. Plus, it's a field where I can make a real impact and help others seek justice.

I couldn't help but feel torn between my own interests and my mom's. It was a tough decision to make, knowing that whatever I do will either make me happy or my mom happy.

"You all will be researching more about the school you want to attend, and if there are any scholarships that come with it, now get to work."

I rested my head on my crossed hands, letting out a weary sigh. Researching schools and scholarships felt like an overwhelming task, and the headache from earlier had crept up on me. It stinks that it chose to strike during this class, skipping entirely the earlier period.

Frustration welled up inside me, and I couldn't help but mutter, "Fuck."

Suddenly, I felt a gentle hand brushing my hair away from my face. Startled, I looked up to see Aiden. Irritated, I snapped, "The hell, I'm really not in the mood right now."

Okay, now I feel bad. I lifted my head and turned towards him, offering an apologetic smile.

"Sorry," I began. "I just don't feel good right now."

Aiden's gaze shifted downward, his expression softening. "Wow, Zhera Thompson is apologizing; that's something new," he remarked, a hint of surprise in his voice.

I couldn't help but scoff at Aiden's remark. "What do you mean? I always apologize when I'm wrong."

He nodded, his voice dripping with sarcasm. "Mhm, sure you do."

I rolled my eyes, realizing he was teasing me. "Okay, maybe not always, but most of the time."

"Wow, Zhera Thompson admitting to something she does—that's new."

"Okay, that's enough." Aiden's laughter filled the air, and I couldn't help but join in. "It's just so easy to tease you, you know."

Shifting the conversation, Aiden leaned in closer, his curiosity piqued. "So, where are you planning to go?" he asked.

I leaned back, contemplating for a moment before revealing my decision. "I'm thinking of going to Yale," I finally shared.

Aiden's eyes widened with surprise. "Yale Law?"

I nodded.Yeah, Yale Law. How did you know?"

He smirked. "I mean, you love to argue, so perfect for you." Hm true.

I tilted my head slightly, twirling my pen between my fingers. "You know, you still haven't told me what you want to be," I reminded Aiden.

It struck me that, despite knowing Aiden for some time now, I never really knew his true passions. Sure, he's good in a lot of subjects like sports, science, and English, but I couldn't pinpoint what truly sparked his interest. It made me wonder what he loved and what he wanted to do in the future.

As I reflected on the past, it became obvious that Aiden was a bit of a mystery. While people knew him for his love of football and his intelligence, there was something enigmatic about him. He kept his true passions and desires hidden, only revealing glimpses of himself to those who were closest to him.

Aiden leaned in closer, his voice filled with a mix of uncertainty. "You really want to know?" he asked.

I nodded slowly.

He slumped back in his chair, a hint of disappointment in his expression. "Honestly, I have no idea," he admitted with a sigh.

Surprised by his response, I leaned forward, wanting to understand more. "You don't?" I asked.

"No, my dad wants me to pursue football, but that's not something I want, you know what I mean?"

I definitely do. With my mom's situation,

"Yes, I do." I stopped playing with the pen. "Wait, why does your dad want you to continue playing football?"

Aiden crossed his arms, his face reflecting a look of contemplation. "Well, you know, the old man wants me to be more like my brother," he explained. "He wants me to continue playing football professionally, just like my brother did."

His brother?

"I th-"

Before I could respond, my teacher's voice interrupted our conversation. "Zhera, you're being called to the office," she called out.

—

I walked into the room, and my steps faltered when I saw Michael seated across from the dean.

"Uh, hey," I stammered.

The dean's face lit up as she stood up, greeting me with a warm smile. "Well, hello there, Zhera. Please, have a seat."

I settled into a chair, stealing a quick glance at Michael, who had a grin plastered on his face. I'm not a fan of that.

"So, Zhera, you're probably wondering why you're here," the Dean began, settling into her chair. "Well, it turns out that Michael here has been struggling with math and is in need of a tutor."

My heart sank. Oh no, this was not what I had in mind.

"Considering you're one of our top students, we thought you'd be the perfect fit," she continued, a hopeful smile on her face.

I glanced at Michael, wondering what on earth he had told them. That dumbass!

"Apparently, Michael mentioned that you two are friends, so that's a bonus," the Dean added, giving us the opportunity to ask any questions.

I took a deep breath, trying to gather my thoughts. This was definitely not the situation I had anticipated, way worse.

The room fell into a heavy silence, as if time itself had come to a halt. I struggled to gather my thoughts, attempting to quell the anger bubbling inside me.

"I have a really packed schedule, miss," I finally managed to say.

The dean's reassuring smile remained unwavering. "No need to worry about that. The tutoring session will only last for an hour and thirty minutes, right here at school. And the best part? You'll be compensated for your time by the school."

"Compensated?" I repeated, slightly taken aback.

"Yes, you heard right. The school highly prioritizes the education of each and every student, so you will be getting paid."

"Um, may I ask how much?"

She chucked "I know you would ask that question; well, it varies; as time goes by, your pay will be from 85 dollars to 100 dollars per session."

I slightly gasped. Wow, that's a good pay. Fuck, what should I do? How would Ciara react to this? It feels super weird.

"I can see you're contemplating; just know that this will be a good look in your college essay."

This is way harder, now that she made my decision harder, it's such a good opportunity, and I need the extra money.

With a weary sigh, I nodded. Quickly regretting my decision.

—

wordcount: 1227

27 | Interest

- -

As I hurried my steps towards the library, my heart pounding with anticipation, I couldn't help but steal a glance at my reflection in the tiny mirror I held in my hand. I wanted to make sure I looked presentable.

Finally, reaching closer to the library, my eyes landed on Aiden. But my mood quickly soured when I noticed him talking with someone—Leigha? She was talking animatedly, while Aiden wore an awkward smile on his face. What was this strange feeling bubbling up inside me?

Taking a breath, I approached the door and cleared my throat to get their attention. "Excuse me," I politely interjected, trying to mask any hint of unease. Then, without dwelling on the situation, I made my way inside the library.

As I reached in, a strange sensation washed over me—a mix of emotions that I couldn't pinpoint. Was it jealousy? No, it couldn't be. I've been jealous before, but this feeling was different—a different type of jealousy, one that was very unfamiliar.

Shaking my head to clear my thoughts, I directed my attention towards the towering bookshelves that stood in front of me.

With a graceful glide of my hand, I ran my fingers along the spines of the books.

It's been a while since I've read. Reading was one of my favourite hobbies. The feeling of reading can be really amazing. It's like entering another world, where your imagination can flourish and you can experience extraordinary things without even leaving your seat.

The words on the page come to life, and you can feel the emotions of the characters. Imagine the places and situations described.

I just can't describe how good it makes me feel, and these past few months, I haven't been reading at all—all the student council responsibilities, the project, studying, events, and so on. I'm a person who usually carries a book around, no matter where I am. So now that I haven't been reading at all, it shows how tired and busy I am.

My face lit up when I found the book I was looking for. 1991's The Cipher; it's a book that's been recommended too.

I eagerly stretched up on my tiptoes, reaching for the book, only to find it placed on a shelf that seemed unreasonably high. Why was it so high? There is no reason for these shelves to be this high.

Before I was about to give up, I felt a presence behind me, and a hand swiftly took hold of the book. Aiden? I could feel my body tense up at the sudden closeness.

I faced him, only to be met with a sly smile. "This is the kind of book you read, Thompson?" he remarked, checking out the book.

I replied with a simple "yeah."

"Not surprised," he quipped, a hint of amusement in his voice.

Feeling the need for personal space, I gently pushed him away, creating a distance between us. With a longing gaze, I extended my hands, silently pleading for the book.

As Aiden handed the book back to me, our fingers brushed against each other, and a subtle sensation coursed through me. It was a weirdly good feeling, one that I couldn't really put into words.

Aiden made his way towards another section of the bookshelf, his fingers gracefully gliding along the row of books. Curiosity getting the better of me, I approached him and said, "You read, too?"

He nodded. "Yeah, most of the time." His gaze shifted towards a particular book, a glimmer of recognition flickering in his eyes.

"All these years that I've known you, and this is the first time I'm hearing about this," I exclaimed, a tinge of surprise in my voice.

Aiden turned towards me, a smile playing on his lips. "Really?" he asked. I nodded, and my curiosity piqued. "Mhm, what kind of books do you even read?"

He scratched his head, pondering for a moment. "Romance," he answered with a sheepish grin, revealing a side of him I had never expected.

Wow, Aiden Miller is reading romance books. I don't know why it even came as a surprise; I mean, it's Aiden Miller.

It seemed so unexpected, yet somehow fitting for him. I tilted my head, a smile forming on my lips. "Romance? I never took you for someone who reads romance," I remarked.I placed my hand on the book. "Is that one a romance novel?"

Aiden nodded. "Yep, I've been searching for this one for some time now."

"What is it?"

He hesitated for a moment before replying, "Gone with the Wind. It's a pretty old novel you probably haven't heard of."

I flipped through the pages, surprising him with my response. "No, I've actually read it once."

He gazed down at me, then lightly shoved me. "I'll let you know how it was then."

Aiden then started making his way to our seat; I couldn't help but be frozen in place. I placed my hand on my chest. Why's my heart beating so fast?

—

As the minutes ticked by, I found myself lost in my own thoughts, barely making any progress. My mind seemed to be elsewhere, completely disconnected from what I had to do.

Aiden miller

My gaze lingered on him, who was sitting across from me. Suddenly, something caught my attention. Had I never noticed how attractive he was before? I mean, sure, I always knew he was good-looking, but in that moment, it was like seeing him in a whole new light.

His eyes—were they always that mesmerizing shade of hazel? And his lips—they looked so soft and perfectly pink. It was as if time had frozen, and I couldn't help but be captivated by his beauty.

In this moment, everything else faded into the background, and I found myself lost in the allure of Aiden. It was like seeing him for the first time, and I couldn't help but wonder if I had been missing out on this breathtaking sight all along.

Why do I see him differently now? In a new light, I mean. I placed my hands on my face. God, this is confusing.

As I sat there, pondering my thoughts, the library door swung open, breaking the silence. In a reflexive response, I turned my head to see who it was. My eyes landed on a tall boy with impeccably braided hair; he looked very confident as he looked around the unfamiliar surroundings.

He seemed a bit lost, as if he didn't belong in the library and wasn't sure what to do next. However, when his gaze met mine, a radiant smile spread across his face, and he made his way towards my table.

"Hello, Zhera!" he greeted me warmly.

—

New character alert! I just realized I barely have any characters in this book. Well, tell me if I should add more. wordcount: 1150

28 | Dumbfounded

A iden let out a snort as I offered an awkward smile and greeted the newcomer. "Um, hi?" I said.

"Oh, my bad for not introducing myself. I'm Xavier, a junior, and I happen to be that guy's friend," he said, pointing at Aiden. His last words caused my eyes to widen in amusement.

"What are you doing here, Xav? This isn't really your scene," Aiden remarked, looking visibly annoyed.

"Very funny," Xavier replied with a grin as he took a seat beside Aiden, his eyes fixated on mine. "I can't believe after all this time I'm finally meeting Zhera Thompson."

I scrunched my nose, wondering why he was making it seem like I was some rare being.

"Not the talkative type?"

"I mean, how am I supposed to respond to that?"

"True, true," he acknowledged with a chuckle. His gaze then wandered around the room before he redirected his attention back to us. "Anyways,

what have you two been working on? Aiden, you've barely been at practice."

He skipped practice for this? I had no idea. "You have practice around this
time?" I questioned, genuinely surprised.

Aiden scratched his head with a nod. "Sometimes I have practice around
this time; nothing too serious."

Nothing too serious? He's skipping his practice for this. But his words
were a reminder that he was, in fact, the type of person who prioritized
his education over everything else, including sports.

I felt a pang of concern, knowing how important his sport was to him.
"Maybe we can start ending it earlier, so you can make it to practice?" I
suggested

He shook his head. "No, it's fine. I like working here instead."

Unwillingly, I nodded. Why was I worrying so much? Normally, I
wouldn't give a damn about him missing practice because of this, but what
the hell is going on with me—has he cast a spell on me?

I then heard someone shift on their chair and say, "This place feels suffocating." Xavier stated as he untied his necktie.

"Don't you have better things to be doing?" Aiden mumbled under his
breath.

Xavier rolled his eyes, then stood up. "Well, it seems like I'm not welcomed
over here; I'll be making my way out."

"finally."

I lightly chuckled. To someone else, these two seem to not like each other at all, but it's obvious they care for each other. After all, Xavier had made the effort to come all the way here just to check up on his friend.

Just as Xavier was about to walk past our table, he suddenly stopped next to me, leaning in and whispering in my ear, "This guy never shuts up about you." With a mischievous laugh, he made his exit, but not before the librarian told him to shut up.

My eyes widened, and a smile slowly spread across my face. Aiden, always observant, noticed my reaction. "What did he say?"

I couldn't help but smile sheepishly and wave my hand dismissively. "Oh, nothing too important."

But Aiden wasn't one to let things go. He leaned back in his chair with a heavy sigh and pleaded, "Come on, if its nothing too important, then tell me."

"I rather not."

"You're really not going to tell me, Thompson?"

I chuckled, shaking my head. "Not a chance." Now I'm left wondering what Aiden has been saying about me.

Three days later

"Are you sure you want to do this, Zhera?"

The question echoed in my mind as I reached for the doorknob. I hesitated for a moment, feeling the gravity of the situation. "No."

I heard some shuffle on the other side of the phone. "You told Ciara, right?"

"Yup, it went surprisingly well, but Ciara is pretty mature, so what did I expect?"

"True, she doesn't get worked up on these types of things; oh yeah, did you notice that these days she's been a bit like herself again?"

"Mhm, it seems like it; I think she's getting over that whole situation."

Suddenly, a familiar voice called out to me, and I turned to see Michael waving me over.

Ending the call with a quick goodbye, I let out a shaky sigh as I approached him, my grip on my bag tightening.

"Hello," I managed to say, trying to steady my nerves.

"Hi Zhera."

I took out the papers from my bag, and after I took a seat, the one further away from me said, "So what do you need help with?"

"Well, since I came a bit later into the semester, I'm having some difficulties catching up. So I basically need help with everything." He admitted it sheepishly.

"Alright, take out your papers, and we can start with the basics," I suggested, trying to keep my tone neutral.

He scratched his head with a nervous chuckle. "So this is where I messed up; I forgot to bring my papers."

Of course he did.

"You forgot to bring your papers to a tutoring session?" I scoffed, struggling to hold back my eye roll.

He responded with a chuckle, "Yeah, I was busy with something—well, someone, to be more specific."

I let out an exasperated groan. I really didn't need to know the details. Then he dropped the bombshell:In fact, the person was someone you know very well."

My heart sank for a moment as I blurted out, "Ciara? You've got to be kidding me."

"Yup! We were, uh, busy, and I lost track of time."

Why would she be with this guy after how he humiliated her at the dance? Not to forget, it wasn't the first time he did something like that.

And I even told her about the things he was saying in class with those girls. Oh my

"Can you tell her to meet me up after this session? My phone died."

Alright, nope, this is where I draw the line. I don't know why he feels so comfortable telling me this or why he has that smile plastered on his face, as if all of this is amusing to him. But that doesn't work for me.

"It looks like there's no point in having a tutoring session today if you're not even prepared, and I don't appreciate you talking about my friend after everything you've done, so if you'll excuse me, I have better things to be doing," I said firmly as I gathered my belongings and left a dumbfounded Michael behind.

As I turned to leave, a whirlwind of emotions swept over me. Was this all a joke to him? Who would have thought that the seemingly kind-hearted guy could be so.. ew?

I quickly dialled Ciara's number, it's time to talk

—

Wordcount: 1116

29 | Talk

As the door creaked open, Miss Daniel grinned warmly. "Hi honey, the girls are upstairs!" Returning her smile, I gave her a hug before making my way upstairs.

Today was the day we planned to pack our suitcases for the upcoming senior trip, which is just a few days away. We had decided to do it together. After the incident with Michael the other day, I called Ciara and asked if we could talk about it while packing today.

As I entered the room, I was greeted by the sight of my friends, all dressed in their pajamas, surrounded by scattered clothes and packing materials.

"Hello, ladies," I greeted them with a warm smile. I was trying to hide my surprise at the mess around the room.

"Hey Zhera!" they chimed in unison, their voices filled with excitement.

My brows furrowed as I glanced around the room. Clothes were scattered everywhere, and by everywhere, I mean everywhere. How did two people create such a mess?

I couldn't help but raise an eyebrow as I picked up one of the clothes from the floor. "Do we really need this many outfits for the trip, guys?" I asked, trying to sound both curious and amused as I made my way to the cozy bean bag chair.

"What kind of question is that, Z? Of course we do," Ciara replied, sounding a bit offended.

"Yeah, I mean, the trip is for like five days, Z, so we need a lot, but not too overboard like Ciara," Khelani chimed in, struggling to fold a shirt properly.

"What's that supposed to mean?" Ciara asked defensively.

"Exactly what I said," Khelani responded with a grin.

I couldn't help but giggle. "What Khelani is trying to say, Ce, is that you're a clothing enthusiast." I playfully raised my finger in the air before she could counter back. "But before you say anything, remember that one trip to France when you overpacked? You had to remove so many clothes and put them in your parents' suitcases."

"Haha, funny."

Khelani giggled. "Yes, very funny."

They both then looked at each other for a moment and nodded. I glanced between the pair. What was that?

"So, Zhera." Ciara began, her voice seeming different than before.

"yea.."

"You know how we're your best friends ever, and you love us so much?" Khelani continued.

"Sure."

"And as your best friends, it's only our job to know what's happening in your love life."

"It is?" I scoffed, knowing where this was going.

"Yes, Aiden. Talk, now."

I shrugged my shoulders, trying to play it cool. "There's nothing to talk about," I said, hoping to brush off their observations.

But they both let out a sigh, exchanging knowing glances. "Come on, we've noticed how you've been lately," Ciara hinted. "You've been happier, smiling more whenever his name comes up, and you get all excited when it's time for your sessions."

My eyes widened. "Was it really that obvious?" I blurted out, quickly covering my mouth in embarrassment.

They chuckled gently. "Well, maybe not to everyone, but to us, it was pretty clear. Just admit it, you like him now. That hate you felt before, it's gone, isn't it?"

I blushed slightly, feeling a mix of nervousness and excitement. It was true; my feelings had changed, and I couldn't deny it anymore.

That left me wondering where all that hate came from and how it managed to grow over time. Maybe it was all those arguments—perhaps the first day we met? or the constant competitions and debates.

Those things used to drive me crazy, but now they're the things I secretly crave whenever I see him. It's like his presence brings me happiness, makes me smile more, and makes me want to spend more time with him. Those were definitely signs of having feelings for someone, right?

"Guys," I said, my voice filled with anxiety.

"Just admit it, Zhera. You like him," they deadpanned, their words hitting me like a reality check.

At that moment, I couldn't deny it any longer. I had feelings for him. But it was so hard to wrap my head around it. How could I be falling for someone who has always rubbed me the wrong way?

"I think... I like him," I finally confessed, my voice filled with a mix of surprise and uncertainty.

And you know what happened next? They both went absolutely wild, cheering and jumping around the room like a couple of crazy people. But then, they rushed over to me, engulfing me in the tightest hug ever.

I couldn't help but hug them back, feeling a mix of emotions swirling inside me. God, I can't believe this. I actually have feelings for Aiden, Aiden freaking Miller. It's like a total shock to my system, but there's no denying it anymore. It's real, and I have to face it head-on.

2 hours later

"Ciara, could we talk now?" I asked as I finally zipped my suitcase shut, letting out a huge sigh.

The room was filled with a pleasant aroma of lavender from the scented candles on the dresser. Khelani was peacefully asleep on the floor, limbs sprawling in every direction.

Now was the time for us to talk about Michael; as much as I didn't want to, we had to.

Ciara nodded understandingly and made her way over to her bed, where I was sitting. She climbed up and hugged her plush toy tightly against her chest.

"So, how do I say this?"

Before I could continue, she spoke up. ""I know what you're about to say, Z, and before you do, let me say something first. I was with Michael a couple of days ago, and I assume that's what he told you."

I confirmed, nodding my head.

Ciara shifted on the bed, sorting her thoughts before continuing. "I was the one who asked him to talk," she said, her voice barely above a whisper. "I wanted to know why he did all those things, like, well, you know."

I nodded, taking in her words. "I see," I said, my voice soft. "So, what did he tell you?"

"He mentioned that he was preoccupied with more important things and considered those things to be immature," Ciara recounted.

That motherfucker. Instead of being honest with her, he chose to ignore her for a whole day and mess with her emotions multiple times.

Ciara's isn't the type to be hung up on guys; she doesn't spend much time in relationships, so if she feels this way, then that means she really did like that repulsive scorn.

I listened attentively, restraining myself from expressing my anger out loud since I know Ciara doesn't like that kind of language.

"So, the things he said about you two kissing were false?"

She paused for a moment, scratching her head. "Sort of. He did try to kiss me when he realized how hurt I was, but I didn't give in."

I raised my hand in the air, giving her a high-five. "Way to go, C!" I exclaimed with excitement.

"Yeah, way to go, Cece!" I heard Khelani's sleepy voice chiming in.

Ciara snorted and asked, "Is she sleep talking?"

Curious, I leaned over the bed to get a better look at Khelani. She was completely knocked out, peacefully asleep. "It seems like she is," I confirmed with a smile.

My mind immediately shifted to Aiden, and a smile just couldn't help but spread across my lips. It's still so surreal to think that I actually like him. Like, seriously, Zhera Thompson likes Aiden Miller? Who would've thought?

As I thought about our upcoming session, my smile grew even bigger. I couldn't help but wish that the weekend would just hurry up and end already.

—

Wordcount: 1299

Feelings have finally been revealed...

30 | Interrupted feelings

As I unpacked my things, I noticed that Aiden wasn't sitting down. "Why aren't you sitting down?"

This is the first time we talked since I realized my feelings. I'm trying to keep things calm and normal.

I couldn't help but wonder what was going through his head as a teasing smile tugged at the corners of his mouth. "Come on, let's go do it somewhere else today," he said, his eyes gleaming.

"Miller, what are you-" Before I could finish my sentence, he took hold of my hands and gently guided me further into the library. His touch sent a shiver down my spine, and I felt a light blush creeping onto my face. Since when did I become so flustered by his touch?

"Where are we going?"

"It's somewhere further into the library, I found recently. Come on."

I never realized how large the library was until we moved farther inside. We arrived at a quiet spot, a comfortable reading nook nestled away from the main path.

This place looked like a hidden gem and provided a place for people who wanted a peaceful escape within the library's walls. It is adorned with cozy floor chairs, soft lighting, and some greenery.

I couldn't help but notice the dim lighting in the room. "It seems a little dark in here," I remarked, attempting to break the ensuing silence.

"It's because this place is tucked away, and it's pretty dark outside right now," Aiden explained, his voice calm.

I took a quick peek around while grinning slightly. "I like it; it's nice," I said, taking in the cozy atmosphere.

"I knew you would," he replied softly, his eyes meeting mine for a second before I quickly glanced away.

"So this is our last session," I muttered, fidgeting with the bracelet on my wrist. Why was I suddenly feeling so nervous?

He shifted closer to me, inching towards me with a gentle confidence. "It is"

"To be honest, I'm kind of going to miss this, just a bit," I confessed, my voice barely above a whisper.

"Just a bit, huh?" he smiled. "Yes, just a bit," I smiled in return.

Aiden crossed his arms. "Well, I'll admit that I'm going to miss it a lot."

"You are?"

"I am. I guess hearing your complaints and insults is something that I'm going to miss," he said with a hint of sincerity in his voice.

I gave him a quick glance, feeling a rush of emotions. "Okay, I'm going to be totally honest, and I know you'll use this against me in the future, but," I waited a moment, noticing a sneer appear on his lips. "I will miss spending time with you like this. much more than I had anticipated."

"I knew you would, and I'm definitely going to use this against you in the future, Thompson."

I rolled my eyes. "Of course you are." He then shifted closer to me. How close was he going to get?

"I'm going to ask you a question, and you have to be completely honest with me, Thompson. Alright?"

"I'll try."

"Do you still hate me?" he asked, his eyes searching mine for an honest answer.

I paused, fiddling with my bracelet, before meeting his gaze. "No, I actually tolerate you now," I replied, trying to find the right words to convey the emotions that I had developed over time.

I couldn't pinpoint exactly when my feelings had shifted, but I found myself enjoying his company more and more. There was a certain warmth and comfort in his presence that I hadn't felt before.

"Zhera Thompson tolerates me? That's new," he remarked with a hint of surprise in his voice.

I couldn't help but snicker at his reaction. "I've never hated you. I just had an unexplainable distaste for your existence. That's all," I explained, shrugging my shoulders casually.

"Wow, that's way better." He joked sarcastically.

"On a serious note, I don't hate you—well, not anymore."

"What changed?"

I paused for a moment, thinking about how to explain it. What did change? Why do I tolerate him now? Why is it that every time I'm around him, my heart skips a beat and I blush at every minor thing?

I'm not sure why I'm asking so many questions, but I know that it's because I like him. I couldn't tell him that, though.

I stopped fidgeting with the bracelet and locked eyes with him. "I don't know; I think I like you a bit more now."

"I like you too."

My heart skipped a beat at that. And a smile formed on my lips—something I've been doing whenever I'm around him.

As we sat there, the dim lighting casting a soft glow around us, I couldn't help but notice how close he had gotten. The air between us crackled with anticipation, and I could feel my heart pounding in my chest.

My heart raced as I found myself lost in his eyes, the world around us seem to be fading into insignificance, leaving just the two of us.

As he leaned in, dazed hazel eyes locked with mine, he whispered softly, "I'm going to miss this too, more than just a bit." His voice was filled with a mixture of longing and tenderness.

Time seemed to stand still as our faces drew closer, the proximity almost unbearable. I noticed his eyes traveling down to my lips then back to my eyes.

A surge of courage washed over me, and I closed the remaining distance between us.

Just as our lips were about to meet, we were interrupted by a sudden voice from across the room.

"The library is closing soon! ten more minutes."

My heart skipped a beat as I jerked back, feeling like a startled deer caught in headlights. The rush of emotions flooded my mind like a whirlwind, swirling with excitement, nerves, and a tinge of confusion.

Was this really happening? Was I actually about to share a kiss with Aiden? My thoughts were abruptly interrupted by the sound of books closing and chairs scraping against the floor as people began to pack up.

Aiden's voice broke through my racing thoughts, slightly muffled as his hands covered his face. "We should get going." I looked up to see his cheeks flushed with a blush.

Without missing a beat, he stood up and offered, "uh, Let me walk you home." His words hung in the air, filled with a mix of awkwardness and genuine concern.

It was kind of cute.

I couldn't help but let out a nervous giggle, feeling a wave of warmth wash over me. "Sure, that sounds nice," I replied, trying to keep my own blush in check.

As we gathered our things and made our way out of the library, there was a blend of awkwardness and shyness that enveloped us.

—

As we walked side by side, our steps slightly out of sync, the air crackled with a sweet, unspoken tension.

I made sure to look straight ahead; I was not about to make any unnecessary eye contact with him, especially not after what was about to happen.

I groaned internally. God, why was this happening to me? Why did I have to like him, Aiden of all people, really?

With each step, the distance between us and my house seemed to shrink, but time also seemed to stretch, as if the universe were playing a gentle game of tug-of-war with our emotions. The streetlights cast a warm glow on our path, adding to the moment.

As we reached my front door, we came to a halt. I hesently turned to face him, our gazes locked.

I waved. "Alright, see you soon, Aiden."

With a nervous smile, I leaned in and placed a gentle kiss on his cheek. The gesture was awkward yet filled with affection.

As I pulled away, I was met with a soft smile spread across his face, and a light blush that crept his cheeks.

Yup, I'm totally whipped.

—

Wordcount; 1350

Had so much fun writting this chapter, especially the last part..!

31 | Perspectives

Aiden's POV

"Fuck," I muttered under my breath, unable to get Zhera off my mind. My mind was flooded with questions. Did she feel the same way? Was I being too forward? Did she want to kiss me too? The uncertainty weighed heavily on my heart.

I kept thinking about the kiss she gave me on my cheek as I brushed my hands over my them. I mean, that had to have meant something. My cheeks get flushed every time I think about it.

"Hey, Aiden, relax," Xavier said, trying to calm me down.

I threw the ball even further, feeling the tension in my body. "Relax?" I repeated

Xavier shrugged. "Yeah, you both wanted it. So what's the problem?"

His words hit me; maybe I was overthinking things. We both obviously wanted it, and she did lean in too. What would have happened if we didn't get interrupted? That damn librarian..

Expressing my feelings for Zhera seemed like an impossible task, and trust me when I tell you nothing is impossible for me.

I was undeniably infatuated with her; everyone around me could tell, but except for her. She had always been the oblivious type.

"I don't know," I whispered as I brought down the football I was tossing.

Alejandro zipped up his bag, "Let's just focus on preparing for the trip. It'll take your mind off of it."

I stood up from the bed. "You know she's going to be there, right?"

"Well, just be yourself. Act like you usually do, and we can talk about it later."

I sighed "You're right."

Zhera Thompson, her name alone evokes a sense of warmth and affection in me. I've known her for so long and longed for her for so long. She's been the only girl that I liked; since the first day we met, she caught my eye with her personality.

Well, maybe because I broke her project, which was obviously an accident, which she still won't understand. As the years passed and we grew older, my feelings for her also grew.

If younger me found out about this—that I was smitten by the unusual girl who wore pigtails—every day, he would definitely laugh in my face.

My heart is always filled with different emotions whenever I think of her, and I can't help but cherish every moment we share, even the bad ones.

In those moments where she looked like she was about to murder me, even with hatred filled in her eyes, she still looked her prettiest.

Xavier inched closer to me, a knowing look in his eyes. "I can tell you're head over heels for her, maybe even in love."

I couldn't help but admit, "I do love her."

It was a moment of realization, as I chuckled at how I skipped over the "liking" stage and dove straight into love. I really do love Zhera.

From the constant arguments and hate to our shared smiles and laughs. Ah, that smile that she hardly ever shows me whenever she's with me. The dimpled smile that makes her look ten times more stunning.

It was in those moments that I realized just how much I had fallen deeply for her.

"Now I understand why you rejected all those girls, even Leigha fucking Windsor and Maria." Xavier shared.

Those girls meant absolutely nothing to me. They're nothing compared to what I feel for her and what I've felt for years now.

Alejandro swiftly zipped up his bag. "Alright, enough of that, Romeo; let's continue."

"Always the heartless one, aren't you?" With a laugh, I shook my head and made my way to my half-packed duffel bag.

Zhera's POV

I've been thinking about it all day, trying to distract myself with reading, going for a freezing cold walk, and even watching Gilmore Girls. But none of it worked; not even Lorelai and Rory could take my mind off of it.

Thoughts of that moment kept flooding my mind. And that kiss I gave him on the cheek...

"Ugh!" I let out a groan and buried my face in my pillow.

Why did I do that? Was it my way of making up for the interrupted kiss? God and that kiss—well, that almost kiss—I felt a smile grace my face at the thought.

"I can't believe I almost kissed Aiden Miller." I muttered out loud, biting my finger. It was obvious that we both wanted that kiss. What would have happened if we hadn't been interrupted?

I for sure wanted to kiss him; I literally leaned in. We were so close to it.

Once I got home, the first thing I did was tell my friends about it.

But as soon as I mentioned it, they completely lost it. I could hear their screams and the sound of them jumping around their rooms.

It was like they were more excited than I was. I tried to form a sentence, but their screams kept interrupting me. After several failed attempts, I had to end the call. We figured out that we could talk once they calmed down a bit.

So here I am, lying on my bed, lost in my own thoughts. I can't help but wonder what I should do next. Should I call him? Or maybe ask him to meet up somewhere? Or should I just keep quiet and wait until we see each other again?

So many questions but zero answers—that's when it hit me.

I sprang up from my cozy bed, slipped on my trusty slippers, and made my way downstairs. There was only one person who could truly listen to me and offer some much-needed advice.

"Hey, dad!" I greeted him with enthusiasm.

I walked over to the kitchen counter, where my dad sat, stirring his coffee with a spoon. His face lit up with a warm smile as he turned to face me.

"Oh, oh. I recognize that look. What's on your mind?" He asked, gently placing his coffee down.

I couldn't help but be amazed by his intuition. "How did you know?" I inquired.

He chuckled softly. "Well, my dear, I've had the privilege of knowing you for seventeen years now. So, I think you can answer that question yourself."

A smile played on my lips as I took a sip of his coffee. "I need your advice, Dad. Let's say hypothetically speaking." I paused for a second, looking at him. "Key word, dad, hypothetically, if you've known someone for years and, well, you've never really been fond of them. But now, suddenly, you start seeing them in a different light. What does that imply?"

He leaned back, contemplating my words. "I think it means that you've developed some kind of liking for that person."

"But what if, you know, there's a part of me that's still unsure?" I trailed off.

"Well, if there's still a part of you that's unsure, it might be worth exploring those feelings a bit more. Take some time to understand why your per-spective has shifted and what it is about this person that's catching your attention now."

I noded. "Wow, you're good, dad. I don't know why you didn't become a therapist."

He chucked, "Maybe in another life, now get some sleep, honey, big day tomorrow."

Oh, shit, I almost forgot. The trip is tomorrow, and I will be seeing Aiden first thing tomorrow. It could not have come at a worse time.

—

Wordcount: 1264

Today we dove deep into Aiden's heart and seen how he's been thinking this whole time!

I hope you guys enjoyed ;)

32 | Morning madness

As I sipped my tea, a yawn escaped my lips, and I adjusted the strap of my pink duffel bag on my arm. The day of our long-awaited trip had finally arrived, and the clock struck 6:00 a.m. sharp. A group of us seniors gathered outside the buses, while the teachers busily prepared everything we needed.

"Man, all I want is to go back home and catch some shut-eye," I groaned, resting my head on Ciara's shoulder.

"I totally feel you," Kehlani chimed in, letting out a loud yawn and resting her head on the other side of Ciara's shoulder.

Ciara chuckled. Being the only morning person in the group, she was always full of energy in the morning.

"We're already here, so there's no going back." She said this as she playfully tapped our heads.

I nodded, lifting my head from her shoulder, and my gaze fixated on the mesmerizing sunrise. The sky was ablaze with hues of soft orange. The first rays of sunlight gently kiss the horizon, casting a warm and golden glow.

The sight was truly breathtaking—a perfect way to start the day. I nestled my head back onto Ciara's shoulder, feeling the comfort of her presence as I nuzzled my hair against her.

"Alright, seniors. I would be doing roll calls now, so quiet down and get ready." The instructor announced.

—

Once the roll calls were done, it was time for us to stow our luggage in the bagging area. As I glanced around, a frown creased my forehead , realizing that a particular someone was missing.

Was he not coming for the trip? I swear he mentioned something about him coming.

With a weary sigh, I made my way through the luggage area. As I waited for my turn, I couldn't help but feel a bit overwhelmed by the amount of stuff scattered around. Did I really pack that much? Or was I just imagining it?

I only brought a duffel bag and a tiny suitcase, which I thought was reasonable. But now that I was struggling to fit everything inside, I couldn't help but groan in frustration. Why was there barely any space? Was I really bringing too much?

As my bag slipped from my grasp, a exasperated sigh escaped my lips. I scanned the area, realizing that there was barely anyone around to help. I couldn't help but think that this was shaping up to be a less-than-ideal start to the trip.

But then, I felt a familiar presence behind me. In an instant, a gentle hand reached out, deftly lifting my bag and effortlessly placing it where it belonged.

"Good morning." Aiden's deep voice greeted

"Morning," I replied, feeling a tinge of awkwardness as I turned to face Aiden, with a light wave.

We found ourselves in an uneasy moment of silence, both of us unsure of what to say or do next. In this brief moment, my gaze couldn't help but wander over Aiden's body. He wore a casual outfit; black sweats and a hoodie, topped off with a black puffer jacket. It was a laid-back and comfortable outfit.

I couldn't help but notice that Aiden was wearing his glasses, which made him look ten times cuter, today. His hair seemed a bit tousled, as if he didn't get much sleep.

Breaking the silence, I cleared my throat. "Anyway, we should start making our way now," I suggested, stepping from one foot to another.

He nodded, assuring me that he would join me shortly. As I stepped onto the bus, I glanced at my ticket to find my seat. "Alright, seat 5A," I murmured to myself.

When I finally found my seat, a surge of delight washed over me as I realized my seatmate was nowhere to be found. With a smile, I settled into the window seat, which, let's be honest, is the best seat on the bus.

Finally, I can finally sit down after standing in the freezing cold for like twenty minutes. The morning rush was basically done now, and I could enjoy some peace for a couple of hours.

As I let out a relieved sigh, the seat next to me suddenly sank under the weight of someone plopping down. I turned my head to see who it was, and my eyes widened in surprise. It was none other than Aiden.

Of all the people on this bus, fate had decided that I would be sitting right next to Aiden. Isn't that just my luck? I couldn't help but feel a twinge of disbelief that I would have to endure a two-hour and thirty-minute journey right beside him. Wow.

Don't get me wrong. I don't mind sitting beside him; it's just that things are a bit awkward and tense between us, so this isn't the ideal situation.

We made eye contact, and both quickly looked away. I noticed him covering his face with his hands. Something Aiden tends to do when he gets shy or flustered, I smiled at that.

1 hour and thirty minutes later

I found myself growing increasingly sleepy. The hours had passed by, and not once did I exchange a single word with Aiden. Our silence hung heavy in the air, the total opposite of the lively chatter of everyone else, even the teachers.

It was like we existed in our own separate bubble of awkwardness.

But then a sound caught my attention. My curiosity piqued, and I stole a glance in Aiden's direction.

To my surprise, he was engrossed in a book. Not just any book, mind you, but the same one we had seen at the library. It was thanks to that book that I found out about our shared passion when it came to reading.

Aiden was deep into his book, with his brows slightly furrowed. He's fully engrossed in the book he's reading, completely lost in the words on the pages.

I can see the intensity in his eyes as he absorbs every sentence, his focus unwavering. The way he holds the book, the light veins on his fingers showing, him leaning slightly forward, and glasses perched nicely on his face He looks hot—very hot.

From the corners of my eyes, I noticed some girls giggling and blushing while staring at him. But he seemed to pay zero attention to them. Engrossed in his book

That brought a smirk to my face and made the two girls scowl at the zero attention he gave them.

Deciding not to bother him any longer, I closed my eyes, letting sleep take over.

—

"Zhera," I heard a muffled sound, gently pulling me out of my sleep. Slowly, I rubbed my eyes, still feeling the heaviness of sleep weighing me down. As I slowly opened my eyes, a smile formed on my lips as I realized I had been using a soft armrest. It was comforting, like a cushion of support under my head.

And the scent that filled my nose was amazing, like soft vanilla.

But then, I heard it again. "Zhera." The voice grew louder, cutting through the haze of my sleep.

Suddenly, my heart skipped a beat as I recognized the name that followed. "Thompson." In an instant, I jolted up, my cheeks flushing with embarrassment as the realization hit me. The armrest I had been leaning on was none other than Aiden's shoulder.

I turned my gaze towards Aiden, our eyes meeting in a moment of surprise.

The air between us felt tensed with a mix of emotions: confusion, realization, and maybe even a touch of amusement. It felt like time had stood still.

My mind raced, thinking of words to break the silence. I could feel my face burning and my cheeks betraying my embarrassment.

In that moment, I managed to stammer out an apology, my voice barely audible.

Aiden's expression softened, a faint smile playing at the corners of his lips. Even during awkward moments like this, he knew how to make it less awkward.

"I was going to tell you that we're almost there; we'll be there in five minutes."

I nodded, "Alright." Fixing my hair. I then started biting my thumb. I did not just sleep on his shoulders the whole time, did I? It was for, like, a good hour. Did I make him uncomfortable? I hope I didn't.

But that sleep felt so good, and he smelled nice too. Lost in my thoughts. I placed my hand on my face. Feeling something in my stomach.

—

Wordcount; 1424

33 | New York

We finally arrived at the hotel, and we had the option to choose who we wanted our roommate to be, so I chose my friends, of course.

The hotel is amazing. It was like stepping into a dream world. As we entered the grand lobby, we were greeted by sparkling chandeliers and marble floors.

The atmosphere was so luxurious, with plush velvet couches and beautiful artwork adorning the walls.

I kind of felt out of place.

Our room was absolutely stunning. The moment I stepped inside, I was greeted by a breathtaking view of the city skyline through the windows.

Kehlani wasted no time and leaped onto the bed, which was adorned with the softest, silkiest sheets and the fluffiest pillows.

"Oh my goodness, I absolutely love this!" she exclaimed, her excitement palpable as she rolled around on the bed.

Meanwhile, Ciara finally managed to make her way into the room, huffing and puffing. "Why is this suitcase so heavy?" she grumbled.

Kehlani and I exchanged looks, trying our best not to say, "I told you so." We rolled our eyes playfully.

"Alright, you guys, gather around," Kehlani beckoned, settling herself gracefully on the bed with a magazine in her hands.

With a pat on the seats beside her, we both joined her, taking our places on either side.

"Now, where should we go first?" she asked, flipping through the glossy pages of the magazine.

The teachers gave us the option of exploring the area for three hours.

"I think we should head to Central Park," Ciara suggested, her fingers tapping eagerly on the picture of the park in the magazine.

"I'm totally on board with that." I nodded, my excitement evident in my voice.

As a first-time visitor to New York, I was eager to explore the whole city. Most people were in their beds sleeping, but there was no way I was going to waste any time sitting and doing nothing.

"I also noticed there's an ice skating rink nearby," Kehlani said, her excitement overflowing. She wrapped her arms around us tightly, causing us to topple over onto the bed with squeals.

—

"Come on, Zhera, give it a shot," Kehlani urged, her eyes filled with determination.

I shook my head.

We were currently at the ice rink, with the skates clutched tightly in my hands, while Ciara and Kehlani were on the ice.

It's been ages since I last skated, and the thought of it sent shivers down my spine.

"Just try it once, that's all," Ciara pleaded, reaching out to take my hand. With a sigh, I reluctantly took a step onto the ice. But, in an instant, my legs betrayed me, causing me to slip.

"Nope, not happening." I quickly retreated, shaking my head vigorously. There was no way I was going to risk face-planting on the ice.

"You guys, go ahead and have a blast. I'll just chill over there," I said, pointing towards a cozy spot nearby.

They exchanged skeptical glances, concern evident in their eyes. "Are you absolutely sure?" they asked, their voices filled with worry.

"We really don't want to leave you alone," Khelani added.

I smiled warmly, assuring them, "Seriously, guys, I'm positive. I don't mind at all. So go on and enjoy yourselves." They let out a sigh of relief and nodded in agreement while I made my way towards the bench.

Taking this chance to finally take the place in. It's as if there's a serene and enchanting beauty that surrounds me. The park, which is already a stunning sight throughout the year, becomes even more beautiful during the winter.

The trees stand tall, adorned with delicate icicles glistening in the soft light, and beautiful Christmas lights.

I spotted Ciara and Kehlani gliding swiftly on the lake, both waving at me when they saw me. Everyone looked happy on their skates: family, friends, and couples. They all looked happy.

It's moments like these that make winter my favourite time of the year. It brings me such a sense of peace, especially since it's my birthday season.

The air was refreshingly crisp, just the perfect temperature—not too cold, just nice. Everything felt so cozy and inviting. In that moment, I felt completely at peace, taking in the atmosphere around me.

As I took a deep breath, savouring the scene, I heard a familiar voice calling my name, one that I eagerly wanted to hear. "Zhera."

My heart raced with anticipation as I turned to my left, and there he was—Aiden, making his way towards me.

"Hi," I said, my voice filled with a mix of excitement and nervousness. Aiden sat down beside me, his smile gentle and warm. Our legs brushing against each other, creating a subtle touch that sent shivers through my body.

"So, you're here to skate?" Aiden asked, his gaze fixed on the skating rink.

"Not me, but my friends."

I couldn't help but notice how Aiden nodded as he rubbed his fingers across his exposed neck. Was he cold? His nose was a shade of pink, and he didn't seem to be fully covered. Suddenly, an idea came.

I slowly reached up and loosened the scarf from around my neck. The fabric was soft against my skin, and I couldn't help but notice the intricate pattern woven into it.

I held the scarf in my hands. Without a second thought, I scooted closer to him, and before he could react, I swiftly wrapped the scarf around his neck.

For a moment, there was a look of surprise in Aiden's eyes, which was quickly replaced with a look of confusion. He reached for the scarf, about to remove it, but I gently placed my hands over his, halting his movements.

"Thompson," he began, "why are you giving me your scarf?"

I met his gaze. "You look cold," I explained.

Aiden's hazel eyes bore into mine, searching for answers. I averted my gaze for a brief moment. "I'm about to head back soon, so it's fine," I reassured him.

He studied me for a moment, his expression softening. Without a word, Aiden reached down and zipped up my jacket all the way to my neck. "Then, you better head soon, okay, Thompson?" he said.

I felt both touched and slightly flustered at the gesture he made, then lowered my head slightly, offering a nod as a sign of agreement.

A moment passed, then Aiden talked, "Can we tal-" Before he could finish his sentence, a voice interrupted us by calling out his name.

We turned to see a guy waving in our direction, accompanied by a group of people. Among them, I recognized Alejandro, Leigha, and a few others who often hung out with Aiden.

Aiden's face twisted into a scowl as he reluctantly stood up. "I have to go now, but we'll talk later, alright?"

Disappointed, I agreed with a slight bob of the head.

As Aiden began to walk towards his friends, my heart sank a little, wanting so spend more time with him.

But just as my disappointment started to settle in, he suddenly turned around, his eyes locked with mine. With a tender smile playing on his lips, he raised his hand and gave me a wave.

In that moment, it felt like time stood still. The soft glow of the setting sun highlighted the warmth in his beautiful eyes, and a gentle breeze tousled his hair.

I couldn't help but return his wave with a shy smile.

I really do like him.

—

Wordcount; 1269

I love the last part of this chapter, hope you guys liked it too!

34 | Winter night

"**W**atch where you're going!." A biker screamed at us. We halted abruptly in our tracks. I forgot how busy this city was.

Ciara sighed in frustration, clutching her shopping bags tightly. "What's with this city?" she exclaimed.

"Welcome to New York." Khelani chuckled, wrapping her hands around Ciara for comfort.

We were currently going on a shopping spree; it's not a New York visit without a shopping hall. The city was twice as busy this time of the year, mainly because of Christmas, which is right around the corner.

Throughout the day, my mind kept drifting back to that moment with Aiden a couple of days ago. It felt like we were on the verge of having a real conversation, but it got interrupted.

I could tell that Aiden wanted to talk about that kiss—well, almost kiss—and honestly, we can't keep pretending like it never happened. The tension between us is palpable, and it's making things very awkward.

Since that day, we didn't get the chance to talk; every time there was an opening, someone had to interrupt us. It was as if the universe had something against us.

I let out a frustrated groan as we plopped down on a random chair we found in the hotel lobby. "Zhera, don't worry; you'll definitely get a chance to talk to him," Kehlani reassured me.

I sighed, feeling like every opportunity we had to have a real conversation just kept slipping away. Kehlani took a sip of her warm drink, braving the cold weather. "Come on, spill the tea! We need more details about that kiss," she teased.

Shifting uncomfortably in my seat, I began to explain, "Well, we didn't actually kiss. It was more like we were about to, but then things got interrupted. And when he walked me home, I gave him a kiss on the cheek."

Both Kehlani and Ciara exchanged a glance, barely containing their excitement. They were about to bombard me with questions, but I got interrupted by the teachers.

"Everyone gather around."

"Ugh, what is it this time?" I groaned, making my way towards him with everyone else.

The teachers explained to us that there was a winter event happening in the heart of the city. So we had to make our way there. It was also organized, especially by the school, for the seniors.

—

We made it to a beautiful winter event, more like a spectacle. The streets are lined with twinkling lights. People are gathered in the town square, where a beautiful ice sculpture display takes centre stage. The sculptures glisten in the glow of colourful light.

As we're heading through the square, we can hear laughter and the sound of ice skates gliding across a nearby frozen lake.

Nearby, there's a market square bustling with activity. Colourful stalls are lined up, adorned with vibrant banners and decorations.

The air is filled with the scents of freshly baked goods, spices, and fragrant flowers.

People from all over the place are gathered there. The marketplace is displaying their wares, from handcrafted jewellery and unique artwork to fresh food and exotic clothing.

The sound of laughter and music fills the air. The market square is illuminated by twinkling fairy lights, casting a warm and magical glow over the place.

The teachers guided all of us to the centre of the stage. Everyone was excited, and talking to their friends, but my eyes wandered to Aiden Miller.

When I landed on him, I realized he was already looking back at me. It caught me off guard, and I quickly looked away, feeling a bit shy.

Moments like this seem to be happening a lot these days. This was going to be a long night.

—

As the night was winding down, it was almost time to head back to the hotel. Everyone looked tired, but they still had big smiles on their faces. The whole thing was like pure magic, and I didn't want it to end just yet.

Suddenly, I felt a tap on my shoulder. When I turned around, I was met with Aiden. I then noticed that he was wearing the scarf I gave him, all wrapped snugly around his neck.

Ciara and Kehlani couldn't help but giggle and then turned away, giving us a little privacy.

"Zhera, can we talk?"

"sure."

Aiden took my hand and led me away from the group, pulling me closer to the marketplace.

"It feels like we can never catch a break, right?" Aiden let out a big sigh. I nodded.

"I know this might not be the best time, but there are some things I want to say."

My heart started racing. Was I ready for this conversation? Definitely not. But hey, sometimes you have to face the tough stuff, right?

Aiden then started gently rubbing my skin, his thumb tracing delicate little circles on the hand that was still in contact with his. It was like he was lost in his own thoughts, not even realizing what he was doing.

I smiled softly, feeling a soft tingle in my body at the touch.

Aiden's gaze finally met mine. "Things have been different since that day." He paused for a second. "I know we both want-"

Before he could finish his sentence, an old, soft voice interjected, interrupting our conversation. "Are you two a couple?" the old woman asked.

Quickly, I responded, "We're n-"

"What is it?" Aiden asked, obviously annoyed by the interruption. I looked at him with a frown.

The lady stared at us, her expression tinged with skepticism, but soon shrugged it off. "There's this discount for couples; you get to have one piece of jewellery, and it can be a beautiful winter gift for the other, all for free!."

Aiden's eyes lit up as he looked at the fancy jewellery on the tray. "I can pick one of these and not pay a single penny?"

The old lady leaned in close and whispered something to Aiden. I strained my ears, but I couldn't catch what she said. Aiden's smile grew wider, clearly excited about whatever secret she shared with him.

Then, he reached out and grabbed a gorgeous crystal hairpin. It had this light blue colour that reminded me of a winter sky. Aiden held it up in front of my face, and I couldn't help but be amazed by its beauty.

As Aiden held the crystal hairpin, I noticed his eyes softening with admiration.

The old lady beamed, her eyes shining. "This piece is truly exquisite, especially when it's worn by a young lady like you."

"Yes, and it's your favourite colour, sweetheart."

I couldn't help but scoff playfully, a smile tugging at the corners of my lips. I reached out and took hold of the crystal hairpin. "My favourite colour, huh?"

Aiden grinned, "Well, I notice that you always seem to have this colour around you," he said.

I smiled, realizing that he was right. Whether it was the clothes I wore or the accessories, this shade seemed to find its way into my everyday life.

It was like a little secret that only Aiden had discovered, and it made the hairpin even more special.

The lady watched us with a smile. It was like she was brought here to make Aiden and I closer; because of this, the awkwardness between us seemed to have disappeared.

She then clapped her hands together and said, "Just because you two are such a beautiful couple, you can get something else."

"I'll get it this time!" I scooted closer to the booth, admiring the jewelry. Aiden chuckled while standing beside me.

My eyes landed on a beautiful bracelet. The bracelet features dainty links made of gleaming silver, delicately intertwined to form a slender chain.

As I gazed at the bracelet, I couldn't help but notice the hazel gemstones adorning it, mirroring the exact shade of Aiden's eyes. A smile tugged at the corners of my lips as I delicately held the bracelet in my hands.

With a gentle tug of his arm, I clasped the bracelet around Aiden's wrist, feeling a sense of satisfaction. "Perfect," I whispered.

Aiden returned my smile, his eyes fixated on the jewelry. "It's beautiful," he murmured. "I'm never taking it off."

The lady nodded approvingly, her gaze shifting from the bracelet to Aiden's eyes. "Those gems are truly a perfect match for this young man's eyes," she remarked.

"Yeah, that's exactly why I picked it."

"Really?." Aiden asked, lightly caressing the gems on the bracelets.

"yeah." Clearing my throat, I suddenly realized that we had been gone for a while. "Okay, we should head back now."

"you're right."

We turned to where the group was, but, to our horror, nobody from our school was there. Like, seriously, nobody.

"oh fuck."

—

wordcount: 1472

35 | Moment

Why did this have to happen? Of all the moments and places, it had to be here and now. I watched as Aiden put down his phone, cursing under his breath. "No call service," he muttered.

Unable to contain my nerves, I began biting my thumb, a nervous habit that I always do in moments like these. It was as if my body was trying to release the tension building up inside me.

"What if they're already at the hotel? Or what if something bad happened? Or maybe they went somewhere far away?" I rambled, my thumb now feeling the pressure of my biting.

Aiden walked over to me, his presence calming. He took hold of my hands, gently rubbing them to soothe my nerves. "Hey, hey. Don't worry. It's going to be okay. They probably haven't gone too far. It's only been a couple of minutes." His voice was reassuring, trying to ease my worries.

"But still, I don't know this city."

"Good thing I do," Aiden replied casually, as if it were no big deal that he just revealed a piece of information about himself.

"You do?"

"Yup, I don't usually share this with people, but I grew up here, it's been a while since I've been back, so I'm not sure where to go next," Aiden admitted, glancing around uncertainly.

"Don't worry, there's a spot nearby where we can wait until we get more information," he suggested.

This is one thing I admire about him; he can come up with a solution in no time, while I was a nervous wreck.

"Alright, lead the way."

—

As we headed towards the cozy little lodge, just a stone's away from the festival, we were glad to find a spot with an awesome view. The place was small but cozy, and we had it all to ourselves. Everyone was at the festival, leaving us with this hidden gem.

We stumbled upon a seating area with a clear roof that let us gaze up at the night sky. I couldn't help but plop my head down on the table and let out a deep exhale.

No distractions, just us and the peaceful atmosphere of the lodge. It was the perfect spot to finally have a real conversation.

"I'll try to call again." Aiden said, standing up. I simply made a noise, too lazy to talk.

My mind kept drifting back to what went down, half an hour ago. My feelings for Aiden just skyrocketed. I saw a whole new side of him. He noticed all these little things about me that even my closest friends wouldn't catch. I couldn't help but feel this deep admiration for him.

When Aiden came back a couple of minutes later, he told me about how there wasn't any signal, but I'd come eventually. It's something that happens during the winter.

"You still didn't tell me about that book you picked."

"Ah, I didn't finish it; school's been too much." He groaned, "College applications, dad pestering me about taking football professionally, the usual."

"Your dad's still on your case about that?"

"Yeah, since my brother went professional, he wants me to follow up."

"Is your brother still playing?."

I remember now that his brother, who was just three years older than us, graduated a couple of years ago and had quite a bit of fame when he went pro in university. But it seems like things have changed since then.

Aiden seemed a bit uneasy. Maybe I crossed a line by bringing it up. He ran his fingers through his hair, clearly struggling to find the right words.

After a moment of hesitation, he finally spoke up, his voice filled with a mix of sadness and vulnerability. 'My brother's not here anymore."

My heart sank as I realized how awkward I made things. How could I have been so oblivious to Aiden's pain? Every time I asked about his brother or his family, he would change the subject. Fuck, It all made sense now.

Aiden not being here during the school elections, which had been the subject of gossip and rumours, for weeks, was due to the loss of his older brother. I was too preoccupied with the student council elections to notice or care. I could have been there for him, for support, even though I disliked him back then.

"I'm sorry to hear about your brother." Offering nice words in moments likes this weren't my specialty but I always tried.

Aiden smiled lightly, "It's fine."

Aiden's POV

Barely anyone knew about this. I'm a very private person and like to keep personal things to myself. Only about three people knew, including Zhera.

I told those who were closest to me and who I deeply cared about, with Zhera being one of the few.

That period of my life was a real struggle. My dad made it even harder by constantly comparing me to my deceased brother and pushing me to take football more seriously.

It felt as if he was trying to replace my brother with me, using me as a substitute. Causing me to lose passion for a sport I once loved so much.

My brother was a great guy. He had it all; he was nice, had good grades, and was athletic. But sometimes, I couldn't help but feel a bit resentful towards him, mostly because of my dad's comparisons.

I looked up at the only person who could draw a smile on my face at the mere thought of them.

As I looked up, there she was, Zhera, biting her thumb. It was something I noticed she did whenever things got awkward or when she was feeling nervous. She sat there, lost in her own thoughts, staring off into space.

When I returned to school during that time, Zhera was the one who unknowingly brought a smile to my face. Just her presence alone made me feel better, like everything would be okay.

She was the only one who didn't ask me a million questions when I came back, and she acted like her regular self. Even though she didn't like me back then, her presence just made me happy.

End of POV

I could feel myself biting my thumb, overwhelmed with guilt for how I treated him during that time. I was so mean, barely acknowledging him, and now I found out that he was going through something so hard.

Ugh, I hate myself so much. I hate you, I hate you, I hate you so so much.

Aiden then interrupted my thoughts: "You know what could make me feel better, sweetheart?"

Before I could respond, his hands reached out towards me, inviting me to place mine in his.

I moved closer, feeling a whirlwind of emotions as our hands made contact. Our fingers delicately intertwined, creating a soft connection. It was a simple gesture, but in the moment, it felt like the world around us faded away, leaving only the warmth of our hands.

"I just realized you always find a way to make us hold hands."

Aiden grinned. "Do I? Well, I just like holding your hands; it's comforting."

How could he say things like that so casually? Not realizing how much those words made my heart race

Suddenly, a peaceful silence enveloped us, unlike the awkward ones we had been experiencing since that kiss.

Just as the silence settled, a phone rang, abruptly breaking the quietness.

—

Wordcount: 1241

36 | Future

We hopped out of the car and watched it zoom away. Now, we were standing in front of the hotel. Ciara had given us the heads-up earlier that everyone had already made their way to the hotel, but the teachers forgot to count us. Can you believe that?

So, the school called us an Uber to get us back to the hotel. And here we were, stepping into the hotel lobby. It was pretty quiet and kind of dark since it was nighttime.

There weren't many people around, just a few scattered here and there.

"Oh Zhera, Aiden! It's such a relief to see you guys safe and sound," exclaimed one of the teachers as they made their way towards us.

With a grateful smile, I responded, "Yeah, we're doing alright. Thanks a lot for giving us a ride."

"Yeah, thanks."

The teacher reassured us, "No problem at all. Now, it's time for you both to get some rest. We still have two more days left on this trip, so make sure to get a good night's sleep."

After exchanging our goodbyes, we parted ways with the teacher.

As we were about to part ways, Aiden gently halted my steps. "Let me walk you to your room. It's dangerous wandering around at night," he insisted.

I nodded appreciatively, feeling a sense of comfort in his protective gesture. We then hopped into the elevator.

Finally arriving at the front of my room, I turned to face Aiden, a soft smile gracing my lips. "See you tomorrow?" I inquired

Aiden returned my smile. "See you, sweetheart,". Before leaving, he leaned down and planted a gentle kiss on my forehead, leaving a lingering warmth.

When I stepped into my room, I closed the door behind me and leaned in on it. Today was officially one of my favourite days. Spending the night with Aiden, discovering new things about him, and just being in his presence made me happy.

As I saw Ciara walking towards me, a smile spread across her face. "It looks like someone's in love," she teased.

My smile widened, but I quickly denied it. "No, I'm not."

"There's no point in denying it, Zhera."

"I don't know what you're talking about. I can't be in love so quickly."

Ciara raised an eyebrow. "Well, maybe you secretly liked him before?" she suggested.

"W-what, you know I hated him for a long time, like years? How could I have possibly been in love with him?"

"You tell me," she said, her voice trailing off as she made her way to her bed. I was left with a whirlwind of thoughts swirling in my head. It was impossible for me to have feelings for Aiden back then; he was the last person on Earth that I could tolerate.

Liking him? No way. It was only recently, after spending more time with him outside of school, that I began to see a different side of him. Slowly but surely, I realized that he wasn't such a bad guy after all.

Maybe, just maybe, there were some lingering feelings deep down inside me all along. And now, those feelings have turned into something more, something unexpected.

I can't believe how myself, from a couple of months ago would react to this. It's unbelievable how much I've changed in just a few months. Zhera Thompson, having the biggest crush on Aiden Miller? I never would have imagined it.

He used to be the last person I wanted to be around, but now he's the first person that pops into my mind no matter what I'm doing.

Life really is strange, isn't it?

—

The past couple of days flew by in a flash, filled with all the usual vacation activities: taking countless pictures, trying delicious food, and going on shopping sprees. You know, all the typical stuff people do while on a trip.

The only downside was that Aiden and I barely had any time to spend together. It felt like we were back at square one, constantly busy with different things, leaving us with little opportunity for contact.

"Zhera, come on, we need to get going," Khelani called out, zipping up her sweater.

I waved my hand absentmindedly, engrossed in my laptop. "I'll catch up with you guys there."

"Are you sure about that?" Ciara questioned

"Yeah, yeah," I assured them. "I've set a timer, so don't worry. You guys go ahead, and I'll meet you there, alright?"

"Don't be late, okay?, and call us when you're done."

As my friends left, I realized it was our last day of the trip. The teachers set up this dinner right across the street, and I couldn't miss it, unfortunately.

Even though I'm on vacation, I didn't want to slack off and do nothing. December is crazy for us seniors, you know, with all those college applications. I can't let this trip put me behind, no way.

I haven't fully made up my mind yet, but I'm thinking of going to law school. My top choice is Yale, and if that doesn't work out, I'll consider Harvard or Stanford. Choosing the school is the easy part, but, man, doing those applications is a whole different story.

My mom still doesn't know about this, and I have no idea how I'll tell her. I can already imagine the screaming, the disapproving looks, and the days of being ignored that will follow up before she finally talks to me.

My mom has always had high expectations for me. Ever since I was like five five-year-old, she has been determined that I should become a doctor. Because most people in our family have pursued careers in medicine, and she hoped that I would too. But: my mother is not a doctor. This has always confused me, because it seems contradictory for her to push me towards a career she did not pursue.

But you know, parents.

As I finished penning the final words of my letter, a sudden knock echoed through my room, disrupting the quiet atmosphere.

"Who is?"

Maybe it was Ciara or Kehlani; they probably forgot something. I approached the door and cautiously peered through the keyhole, only to be taken aback by the sight that greeted me.

It was Aiden, standing there with a grin spread across his face. I quickly opened the door.

"Good evening, sweetheart."

"Hi?"

"Your friends told me you'd be here, so I came to pick you up, walking alone at night is very dangerous, you know?"

I sceptically looked at him then shrugged.

"Well, I was just finishing up my college apps. You can come in and wait if you don't mind." I opened the door wider, gesturing for him to come on in.

Once we stepped inside, Aiden leaned against the door frame, and as I made my way towards the closet, I searched for a good sweater to wear. I already had nice pants, so all I needed was a sweater.

"You're working on college applications? did you decided which university you're picking?" Aiden asked while loosening his hoodie.

"Yeah, I'm thinking of going to Yale Law as my top choice," I replied, excitement tingling in my voice.

Aiden nodded "Yale Law? I thought you said you were thinking of going into medicine."

"Well, that's what my mom wants me to do, not something that I feel like doing."

Aiden scoffed. "Reminds me of a particular someone." I smiled and said, "I guess our parents aren't too different from each other after all."

It seemed like Aiden and I had our fair share of similarities when it came to our parents, both of them wanting us to pursue something we didn't want to.

"Have you talked to your mom about it?" Aiden asked.

I zipped up the soft, warm sweater in a beautiful shade of baby blue. It was slightly oversized, perfect for the cold. "Nope, and I'm not ready at all."

"You'll be fine; just be straightforward, like I was yesterday."

"So, you told him yesterday? How did it go?" I asked, raising an eyebrow curiously.

Aiden scratched his head and looked around, a hint of uncertainty in his eyes. "Not too bad; he's just been a bit MIA lately, but I think he'll get over it."

I giggled at his response. "Hopefully he comes around soon."

—

As we exited the hotel, a sigh escaped my lips. "Am I the only one who doesn't want to go?"

Aiden turned towards me, his expression mirroring my feeling. "Nope." A mischievous smile then spread across his face, and I could tell he had an idea.

"Wanna go somewhere else?"

—

Wordcount: 1443

37 | One touch

"**M**iller, where are you taking me?" I asked, stumbling on the tree branches.

"You'll see." He responded, guiding me through the leaves.

We're currently walking through this forest-like place. The place was still somewhat lit by the sky, despite it being rather dark.

Earlier, when we left the hotel, we decided to skip the diner and go somewhere else. I made sure to inform my friends so they wouldn't worry. They mentioned that the teachers were too preoccupied with their own activities to notice, and some other students weren't there, wanting to do something more enjoyable on their last day.

"My legs are killing me," I complained, feeling the exhaustion taking its toll.

He smirked. " I can carry you if you need."

I chuckled and replied, "I'm good. Just give me a heads-up when we get there."

With a mischievous grin, Aiden came to an abrupt halt, causing me to bump into him. "We're here," he announced, his excitement evident.

I furrowed my brow and started to speak, but he swiftly moved aside the leafy curtain, revealing a sight that left me speechless.

There was a beautiful, huge lake; it was almost crystal-like. The lake, partially frozen, glistened under the moonlight, creating a mesmerizing view. But that wasn't the best part; behind the lake in the background was a beautiful waterfall, a small one gracefully cascading down icy rocks.

I was surprised to see that the water was still flowing despite the cold; it created delicate icicles that hang from the surrounding branches.

"Aiden, this is-" I couldn't find the words to describe this place. "How did you-"

Aiden gently took hold of my hand and led me to a small bench that offered the perfect point to take in the breathtaking view. "I told you I lived in New York for most of my life."

"Yeah, but still, how did you even find a place like this?"

Aiden let out a sigh, his smile filled with nostalgia. "My brother used to bring me here whenever things got tough with our dad. It became our sanctuary, a place to get away from all the chaos. I guess it's a piece of my past that I wanted to share with you."

I smiled, interwitting my hands with his "Well, it's beautiful."

There was a silence that enveloped us, only broken by the distant sound of a gentle breeze rustling through the branches.

The sky above is like a canvas of deep blues and purples, adorned with countless stars. Their reflection shimmered on the calm water, creating a breathtaking mirror-like effect.

It's a moment of pure serenity where time seems to stand still, and I can't help but be in awe of the beauty that surrounds me.

I hesitated for a moment, my voice barely above a whisper. "Aiden"

He responded with a gentle "hm."

"Did you ever feel any hatred towards me?" The question had been lingering in my mind ever since that moment at the library when he asked me the same.

There was a brief silence, the weight of the question hanging in the air. Then Aiden spoke softly. "Not hate. The emotions I had were similar to what you felt, but they didn't linger for as long."

"Really?" I've always had a feeling that Aiden never truly hated me like I did to him; he would just annoy me and try to get on my nerves.

He hummed, "Yeah, my feelings turned into something else, something more." Something else? What did he mean by that?

"Something else?" I repeated, tilting my head to the side, waiting for him to explain what he meant.

With a heavy sigh, Aiden finally mustered the courage to express his feelings. "I don't know if I can bring myself to say it, but at first I didn't like you," he began, his voice cracking with emotion. "But as the years went by, knowing you more and seeing how you truly are under that cold exterior, my feelings changed."

He took a deep breath, his heart racing with anticipation. "All I'm trying to say is that... I love you, Thompson," he confessed, his voice barely above a whisper.

My eyes widened as Aiden's words hung in the air. Aiden's cheeks flushed with a mixture of embarrassment and hope as he awaited my response.

The place fell silent as I processed Aiden's confession. After what felt like an eternity, my lips curled into a soft smile. "I never expected this," I whispered softly.

Our eyes locked, and the emotions between us were palpable as we sat there, frozen in time.

Without missing a beat, I leaned in and gave him a soft kiss on the lips. It was a gentle moment, filled with the warmth of my affection. But as I pulled away, a surge of emotions overcame Aiden and pulled me back into his embrace. His kiss was more passionate.

Aiden's touch was gentle yet filled with passion, his arms sliding into my hair slowly. With one hand, he pulled my body closer to his, deepening the kiss. The warmth of his embrace enveloped me, making me feel safe and loved. Every brush of his lips against mine sent delicious shivers down my spine, and I found myself melting into his arms.

Our lips were soft and warm against each other, making the cold around us disappear. I felt Aiden's fingers sliding down to lightly grasp my waist.

After what felt like an eternity, I finally broke the kiss, our chests heaving up and down and our breaths mingling in the air. I was too nervous to look at him, so I placed my head in his chest.

"I feel the same way, Miller."

Aiden was silent, as if he were thinking of how to respond. I looked up at him, ready to hear him speak, but he surprised me with another kiss. This time, his lips ventured down to my neck, causing a shiver to run through my entire body.

"I've always wanted to do this," he whispered against my neck, his eyes brimming with a mix of excitement and embarrassment. His cheeks turned a rosy shade, and I couldn't help but let out a laugh.

"Are you blushing?" I asked, unable to contain my amusement.

Aiden's face lit up with a wide smile, and he quickly covered it with his hands. "No, it's just the cold," he replied, trying to play it off.

"Oh, really?"

He gazed down at me, a smile lighting up his face. "Yes,". I couldn't help but return his smile, leaning in for another kiss. But just as our lips were about to meet, a single droplet landed on my nose.

I pulled away, my hand instinctively reaching up to touch the substance. It melted instantly. "Snow?" I questioned, a hint of surprise in my voice.

"Yeah, it's snowing."

My eyes widened as I took in the breathtaking sight. Fluffy snowflakes floated gracefully from the sky, twirling and sparkling as they descended. They gently covered the ground, creating a soft,blanket that transformed the entire place.

"It looks so beautiful," I murmured, turning back to Aiden, who was already looking at me with admiration. "You're right , it's absolutely mesmerizing,"

He came closer. "And happy birthday, sweetheart."

—

Stop why is he making me blush so hard, I had so much fun writing this chapter and kept on squealing the whole time

Anyways hope you guys enjoyed!!

Wordcount; 1243

38 | The truth

He came closer, but his movements were slower. "And happy birthday, sweetheart," he whispered, a warm smile playing on his lips.

I paused for a second, a mix of surprise and realization washing over me. I reached for my phone and checked the time.

12:01, December 15.

Oh, it looks like it's my birthday. I couldn't believe I had forgotten. "I totally forgot about my birthday," I admitted.

Aiden raised an eyebrow. "You forgot about your birthday?"

I nodded. As I grew older, I realized that I didn't put as much care into my birthdays anymore. It just felt like any other day, without the same excitement and anticipation.

Aiden, understanding, stood up and extended his hands towards me. "Well, let's start going then. We've been here for a while now."

I got up, said bye to the place, and then we left. Oh, I can't wait to tell the girls.

—

"So let me get this straight: you guys went to this beautiful magical place, and then he confessed his feelings for you, and you kissed him?"

"Basically yeah." I shrugged with a smile, then ran my fingers on my lips. All I could think about was the feeling of his lips on mine and how we kissed for what felt like an eternity.

There was silence for a moment, then they both burst into squeals. Jumping around the room, holding each other's hands.

Suddenly, they were pulled back to reality by the sound of an angry voice coming from the other room. "Hey, keep the noise down over there!" someone shouted.

We all looked at each other in shock and then burst out laughing. Khelani shouted back, "Sorry!" and eagerly joined me. Ciara came over from the other side. "So, are you two officially dating now?"

My mind went blank for a moment. Dating? Are we actually dating? We didn't really discuss that part. We just confessed our feelings and kissed. But if two people express their feelings and share a kiss, doesn't that usually mean they're dating?

I hesitated and replied, "I guess so."

Kehlani crossed her arms and asked, "What do you mean, 'I guess'?"

"Well, we never really had a proper conversation about it, so I'm not entirely sure." Both Kehlani and Ciara let out exasperated sighs.

"Wait, when he confessed his love for you, how did you respond?" Ciara asked.

"I told him I felt the same way."

"Oh, Zhera, what were you thinking?" they both exclaimed in disbelief.

"What's wrong?"

Ciara shook her head and said, "When someone tells you they love you, you should say 'I love you' back, you know?"

I shrugged. "Oh, I'll just tell him next time we see each other." I hope that didn't hurt him. I'm not too big on sweet words like that.

Kehlani gently squeezed my hand. "What would you do without us?"

I smiled and replied, "I don't know, but I'm grateful to have you both by my side."

They smiled, then hugged me. "Happy birthday, Z! We love you so much."

—

I let out a weary sigh as I stumbled through the doorway, the darkness enveloping me. With a reach, I fumbled for the light switch, hoping to bring some brightness into the space.

And then, in an instant, a burst of sound filled the room as my dad's voice pierced the silence, exclaiming, "Surprise!" There he stood, holding a confetti popper in his hands that seemed to be malfunctioning.

"Give me a moment, honey," my dad said, determined to make it work, as he tapped and shook the popper in an attempt to coax it into action.

A smile spread across my face as I walked over and embraced my dad tightly. "Thank you, dad," I whispered. He was the only reason that I was excited to come home.

On my birthdays, my parents usually had work. However, my dad always made an effort to miss it or come home early. My mom, on the other hand, would often arrive later, regardless of the circumstances.

My dad hugged me back and said, "You're welcome, honey. I can't believe you're already an adult."

The reality of being 18 years old and officially an adult feels surreal. It's like time has flown by, and now I'm on the cusp of going off to university.

"I got you your favourite cake, velvet," my dad continued. "And don't worry, your mom will be home soon. She's just caught in traffic."

Deep down, I knew that the traffic excuse was just to make me feel better. It seemed like she would be late, as usual. But I held onto hope that she would come home soon because I had something important to tell her—the law school thing.

"Thanks, dad," I replied, feeling a mix of gratitude and anticipation. "I have something important to tell you, but I want to wait until mom is here."

My dad looked at me skeptically and then nodded. "Alright."

The birthday went well; we spent most of our time eating some takeout, then watching a bunch of Christmas movies. As the night wore on, I found myself leaning my head on my dad's shoulder, feeling a comforting sense of warmth. He had dozed off, peacefully lost in dreamland. I couldn't have imagined a better 18th birthday.

"Dad, you know that guy? Aiden was his name. Well, during the trip, things happened, and I realized how amazing a person he is."

I was met with snoring, louder this time.

"He makes me feel good about myself, and every time I'm around him, my heart can't stop beating. I think I really do love him, but I don't know how to tell him properly."

I glanced at my dad, who was still snoring away, oblivious to my words. "Do you have any advice for me?" I asked with a chuckle.

"I know from that look you gave me the other time when he came over, you knew something was up."

Just then, the front door swung open, and my mom walked in, looking visibly tired. "Hi, mom," I greeted her.

She paused for a moment, her confusion giving way to a warm smile. "Happy birthday, Zhera," she said, masking her weariness with genuine joy.

I got up to help her with her bag. Placing it on the kitchen counter, she made her way. "Thank you, mom."

"Mom, there's something I need to tell you. Can you promise not to be mad?" I asked, my voice trembling slightly.

She raised an eyebrow, her curiosity piqued, but reluctantly nodded. "Alright, if you put it that way, what is it?"

I started fiddling with my fingers. Was I feeling so nervous to tell my mom this? At the end of the day, this is my life, and I won't let her dictate what I want to do. With all the courage left in me, I took a deep breath in

I continued fidgeting with my fingers, trying to steady myself. Finally, I took a deep breath and let it out slowly. "I want to go to law school, specifically Yale Law. And if that doesn't work out, Harvard and Princeton are my backup options. I really hope you can support me in this decision and won't be angry with me," I blurted out, feeling a sense of relief after getting it off my chest.

There was a silence—an awkward one that I hadn't experienced in quite some time. "Mom?" I called out, hoping for a response.

"Wow, you're not kidding? You're being serious right now?."

Oh God, this was not the reaction I expected. "Yes, mom, I'm being serious; I've always wanted to be one, not a doctor."

She sighed "Fine, do what you want. But you're not going to make any money, and you'll be miserable. You should be thinking about getting a real job, like being a doctor or an engineer. Those are the only fields that matter."

I felt a wave of sadness wash over me. Why would she say something like this? Most parents would be supportive, not a bitch about it.

"Mom, why would you say that? A lawyer is just as important as any other profession. I've worked hard to get where I am, and I deserve the right to pursue my dreams, not what you want me to do."

She then tightly crossed her arms and said, "I've done everything for you. I got you into the best schools, and this is how you repay me? By choosing a career path that I don't approve of? I'm just disappointed, that's all."

"Mom I-"

"I'm just disappointed, that's all." She then shook her head and walked away.

I felt my breath hitch. "What the fuck, man?"

Just then, my dad's voice was heard: "What's with all the noise?"

—

Wordcount: 1471

39 | Late night

I went upstairs to my room. I was not about to let her make me cry; nope, not today. We've always had fights, but not ones like this. How could a parent not support their own child? It makes no sense.

I wanted to be far away from here right now. I reached for my phone and dialled the number of the one person who could always make me feel better. After a brief ring, Aiden's deep voice greeted me with a warm "Hello, sweetheart!" Instantaneously, a smile spread across my face.

Aiden picked up on my feelings right away. "What's wrong? You don't sound like yourself."

I let out a sigh, realizing that my feelings were more transparent than I thought. "It's just my mom. I told her about my decision to go to law school, and now she's really upset with me."

"You went to talk about it?" Aiden asked

"Not really," I admitted, feeling hesitant to go into the details. "But I want to see you. Are you busy right now?"

I could hear some movement on his end. "Not at all. Wait for me outside your house, and I'll come pick you up."—

As I sat on my doorstep, I felt a sense of relief wash over me. Being outside, away from the tension in the house, already made me feel a bit better.

Suddenly, I spotted Aiden, slightly out of breath, making his way towards me. He was jogging lightly. "Thompson, I'm here!" he called out, a mix of excitement and exhaustion in his voice.

I couldn't help but laugh at the sight of him. "You look like an idiot right now," I teased, unable to contain my amusement.

Aiden's face was flushed, and his nose was a shade of red from the exertion. But despite it all, he approached me with a warm smile. Leaning down, he gently planted a kiss on my lips, his hands tenderly running through my hair.

I pulled back, but he gently pulled me back in, deepening the kiss, his free hand making its way to my neck, tracing small circles.

"Zhera, you forgot your co-" My dad's voice abruptly halted, and I quickly pushed Aiden away, scrambling to my feet and wiping my lips.

"Oh, dad," I sighed, feeling a mix of embarrassment and frustration.

"Good evening, Mr. Thompson," Aiden greeted my dad with calm composure. How was he so calm after my dad walked in on us practically making out?

"Well, good evening, Aiden. I didn't expect our reunion after all these weeks to be like this," my dad remarked.

Aiden chuckled awkwardly. "Sorry, sir."

My dad nodded and then turned his attention toward me. "Here's your coat, Zhera. Just make sure you don't stay out too late. It's getting dark." He then looked back at Aiden and added, "Keep her safe, please."

I couldn't help but feel a sense of relief. I don't know why I thought my dad would totally flip out, even though he's not the kind.

I threw on my coat, and we started walking, not really sure where we were headed.

"You still don't want to talk about your mom?" Aiden asked.

"Nah, not right now. I just want to forget about her.".

We continued walking in silence, enjoying each other's company. The air was getting colder every day, a sign that Christmas was just around the corner, my absolute favorite holiday. My birthday was also coming to an end soon, with only two more hours left.

This birthday was different from the ones before. Usually, I'd just hang out with my friends or chill at home. But today, I did so many different things throughout the day.

I kissed Aiden, spent the evening with my dad, got into a fight with my mom, and now here we are, taking this walk together. I mean, are we even officially a couple? We never really talked about it. But, like, aren't we automatically dating since we confessed our feelings and kissed? Or am I just overthinking things?

Aiden suddenly let go of my hand, and I watched as he made his way over to the park's bench. I followed him, wondering what he was up to.

As I got closer, I saw him crouching down, his eyes filled with excitement. My curiosity piqued, so I approached him cautiously. And then, to my surprise, he revealed the reason for his excitement—a tiny, fluffy cat nestled in his hands! Its fur was a beautiful mix of colours, and its bright eyes sparkled with mischief.

"Aww!" I couldn't help but exclaim as I extended my hand to gently stroke the soft fur of the adorable cat. However, our cute little moment took an unexpected turn when the cat suddenly hissed at Aiden and attempted to paw at his face. Aiden quickly let go, and in a surprising twist, the cat jumped onto my arms instead.

"It seems like animals aren't really fond of me," Aiden sighed, shaking his head sadly at the situation.

With a playful giggle, I reached over to fix his hair and reassured him, "Your face probably irritates them."

Aiden rolled his eyes and sarcastically replied, "Wow, that makes me feel so much better."

I shrugged.Hey, your face irritates me sometimes too."

He chuckled "But you're the one who fell for this face." I rolled my eyes and said, "Whatever." But then, with a warm smile, he surprised me by planting a gentle kiss on my cheek. To our surprise, the cat hissed at him, leaping out of my grasp and darting into a nearby bush.

"Wow, it really does not like you."

—

As the night went on, we were just having a good time, talking about random stuff, and laughing our hearts out while we strolled around the park.

Eventually, we found ourselves at the swings, and I couldn't resist the temptation to hop on one. The gentle back-and-forth motion made me feel so relaxed, but I could tell that both Aiden and I were getting pretty tired. It was getting closer to the end of my birthday, with only about 10 minutes left.

"Miller, are we a couple now?" I could feel him freeze in his tracks, his movements coming to a halt.

"I guess we are," he replied, scratching his head. "I wanted to ask you to be my girlfriend, but I just couldn't find the right moment yet."

A smile spread across my face as I reassured him, "It's okay, really." He let out a frustrated groan and reached for my hand. "I wanted it to be more romantic than this."

I gently squeezed his hand and said, "Miller, it doesn't have to be all fancy and romantic. I really like how things have turned out tonight, and you've made my birthday so much better."

He grabbed my hands and pulled me into a hug. "I totally did, didn't I?" he said with a confident smirk. "I really am amazing."

I groaned badly and pushed him back. "Let's not get too ahead of ourselves, now."

Aiden pulled me closer, wrapping his arms around me in a tight embrace. We stood there in silence, but it was a silence filled with warmth and affection. It was one of those heart-melting hugs where you could feel all the love and happiness in the world. In that moment, I knew that being together was all that mattered.

And just like that, my birthday ended in the most beautiful way.

—

Wordcount: 1253

40 | Rumours

"Aww, look at the love bird," Kehlani cooed as I made my way to my locker.

Ciara greeted me with a tight hug, her excitement evident. "So, how does it feel to have a boyfriend?" she asked eagerly.

I shrugged nonchalantly, trying to downplay my emotions. "It's fine."

"You don't have to pretend anymore, and you know? Everyone's been buzzing about you two," Ciara said.

"Why? What's the big deal?"

Ciara's tone became more animated as she explained, "Well, think about it. The two top students of our school, who used to constantly argue, are suddenly getting along and even going places together on the trip. It's kind of a major deal."

"Yeah, like one of those adorable romance stories," Kehlani smiled, lost in her daydreams of love stories she adores.

Ciara and I started giggling at her useless ass fantasies

"You guys can laugh all you want, but don't forget, I was your number one supporter. I just knew there was something special waiting to bloom."

I placed my hands on her shoulders "Alright Thank you, Kehlani."

Changing the subject, Kehlani asked, "So, where is he? I thought you guys would be strolling in hand in hand through the front doors."

I scoffed. "I'd rather be caught dead than do that."

I'm not really the touchy-feely type, you know? private kisses and hugs are fine, but at SCHOOL? no way in hell. It doesn't matter how much I love him, I would never do that.

"Oh our Zhera never the affectionate type, Aiden is strong."

"What's that supposed to mean."

They both laughed while making their ways to class "oh nothing, enjoy your day!"

—

I hurriedly made my way to the bathroom, clutching my stomach in pain as my period decided to make its grand entrance on a Monday. What a wonderful life I have, right?

I've been hiding out in here for a few minutes now, gently rubbing my stomach to ease the discomfort. Suddenly, I overheard some voices, probably three or four girls entering the washroom.

"Did you guys hear about how Leigha was practically glued to Aiden the entire senior trip?" I heard one voice say.

Being the curious person that I am, I stayed quiet and listened in. Hey, don't judge me. When I heard my boyfriend's name and someone else mentioned, of course, I couldn't resist eavesdropping.

"Yeah, I mean, she's cool and everything, but it did seem like she was craving attention, you know?"

" Can you blame her, tho? Aiden is seriously smoking hot. I mean, I might do the same thing."

They all burst into laughter, and for a moment, I couldn't help but scrunch my face in annoyance. But then I took a deep breath and calmed myself down.

"It's so obvious that he's not into her, but she just can't seem to take the hint. It's honestly embarrassing. And let's not forget, everyone knows he's completely obsessed with Zhera."

My heart skipped a beat as I heard my name being mentioned. I froze in place, not wanting to miss a single word.

"Oh, you mean that smart girl? I've seen her in the halls before. She's cute, I can totally understand why he's so obsessed with her."

A smile spread across my face, unable to contain my joy. After a few seconds, they changed the subject and left. It dawned on me that I shouldn't have been eavesdropping in the first place, and a twinge of guilt washed over me.

I've always had my doubts about Leigha, She seems really nice and all, but it's pretty clear that she has feelings for Aiden. I've only seen them talk a few times, but he never really seemed that interested.

Now, the question is, should I talk to him about it? Or should I just let it be? It's just strange how she's always hanging around him, even though it seems like he's not into her.

But it's only normal for me to feel this way right? and if it's something that's constantly on mind so I should talk to him. Getting up and making my way out of the bathroom, I knew where I had to go, where Aiden was.

—

I pushed open the door to the indoor football practice facility, where Aiden was currently hanging out. Earlier, I had texted him, letting him know that I was coming to see him.

Inside, there were about five guys, including Aiden. I spotted him a little further down the group, pacing back and forth. When his eyes met mine, a smile instantly lit up his face, and he made his way over to me.

"Hey, I brought you some water," I said, handing him the bottle. He took it from me, planting a kiss on my forehead before taking a long drink.

"Thanks, sweetheart"

"Break time!" their coach called out, and the guys began to make their way towards the door. As they passed by, they all chimed in unison, "Hi Zhera," with giggles, before heading out.

I furrowed my brows, feeling a mix of confusion. "Don't pay attention to them," Aiden chuckled, gently taking my hand and guiding me to some nearby seats.

"Isn't football season basically done? Why are you guys practicing?"

"Ask our coach, he doesn't care and is making most of us practice more because of the days we missed during the trip," Aiden explained, shrugging his shoulders.

I nodded "So I won't see you as much?"

He smiled then reached out to give me a hug, but I playfully recoiled. "Ew, no, you're sweaty."

He chuckled and reached out to give me a hug again, this time pretending to wipe off his sweat with a dramatic flair. "Don't worry, it's just a couple of days a week, i'll find some time to see you, you know I always do" he reassured me.

"yeah I know." I whispered

Aiden gently tilted my head up, "Something on your mind?"

I couldn't help but wonder how he knew something was bothering me. Was I that obvious? My fingers started fidgeting as I tried to gather up my thoughts

"Well, there's this thing I wanted to ask you about," I finally managed to say." Did you hear about the rumours?"

Aiden's eyebrows shot up in confusion. "There are so many rumors around this school, which one are you talking- ?" He paused for a moment and then his expression changed. "Oh, you mean her?"

If by "her" he meant Leigha, then yes, I was talking about her.

"Yeah," I replied, confirming that that his guess.

Aiden's demeanor shifted slightly, as if he knew exactly what I was referring to. "Oh, you mean Maria? She's just an old friend, our families are pretty close," he explained.

I quickly interrupted him, "I wasn't talking about Maria. Whoever she is, Im talking about Leigha."

Aiden's expression changed again, this time with a hint of recognition. "Leigha? Oh, her. Well, she's not really someone significant to me. She asked me out once, but I turned her down. That's all there is to it. you think there's something more going on?"

I shook my head, trying to reassure him. "not really. It's just that I've noticed she's always around you, and it made me wonder."

Aiden let out a small sigh, his expression showing a mix of understanding. "Yeah,she doesn't seem to take 'no' for an answer very easily. don't worry, if she tries again, I'll be more direct and firm with her."

"alright."

A smirk then formed on Aiden's lips "Were you jealous, Thompson?"

Surprised by his question, I quickly sat up, my voice filled with annoyance. "Jealous? Why would I be jealous? Aiden, you—" But before I could continue my rant, he interrupted me with a warm, comforting hug.

He held me tightly, his voice gentle and reassuring. "You don't have to worry about her or anyone else. They hold no importance to me compared to you, okay?"

I felt a mix of emotions, relief flooding over me as his words sank in. Aiden's gesture and words made me realize just how much he valued our relationship. I couldn't help but smile.

"Maybe I was a tiny bit jealous."

"just a bit huh?"

Yeah, just a bit.

—

Wordcount: 1376

41 | Resolution

Today was the day, I was going to talk to her. Things between me and her had been super awkward and tense lately, and even my dad couldn't stand it anymore.

So there I was, being dragged by my dad into the living room, where she was perched on her throne - aka the kitchen seat. I couldn't help but notice her fingers flying across the keyboard, almost like dragon claws. And those glasses of hers, sitting low on her nose. She was like a beast in human form.

"alright Zhera, go on." My dad said snapping me out of my thoughts

I cleared my throat and made my where towards where my mom was sitting, on the kitchen counter.

We stayed there in silence one not wanted to back down. Either she was going to be the adult.. well the older one and parent and talk or we're not going to be progressing here

"Hunny talk to Zhera."

Yeah mom talk to your daughter.

My mom stopped typing, turned towards him than me. And took a big breath in. "I guess it's been a couple of days since, last time, want to talk about it?"

"yeah." I whispered

I could feel dad smiling.

"I've had some time to think and realized that I was a bit too much that day."

A bit? yeah right, I nodded and stayed quiet, waiting for her to continue, but she didn't of course.

"Do you support my choice?"

"not really, but I realized it's your life and do whatever you want, i'm going to try to understand it."

"But why"

"why what?"

"Why don't you support my choice to be a lawyer"

My mother's response was swift and firm. "Because I sent you to school to be something better, not a lawyer. Your education is important, and a doctor is better."

I felt a surge of frustration and confusion. "School, school, school, that's all you guys talk about," I muttered under my breath.

"What are you talking about, young lady?" my mother demanded, her voice rising. "What do you mean, Zhera?" my dad chimed in.

I guess this was the day that I was going to talk to them about it.

"I feel like you guys always prioritize my education. I also think that my education is important, but sometimes it feels like you guys put it above me."

The room fell into silence, and then my dad broke it with a gentle voice, "How long have you been feeling this way?"

"For a long time, especially during moments like these. It's always about school, school, school. It feels like you never ask how I'm doing or if I'm okay, just about my education ."

The relief flooded through me as I finally let it all out. It felt liberating to express how I felt

My mom turned towards me a look of regret on her face. "Why didn't you tell us earlier?"

I fiddled with my fingers "I don't know, I just didn't know how to tell you."

She looked at my dad, and he sighed.

"Sorry, for making you feel that way, hunny." He said .My mom continued "We never wanted to make you feel like that, of course we care about you and you will always come first okay?."

Wow they were really apologizing, especially my mom. I never knew this day would come

"okay, and i'm sorry for not wanting to be a doctor."

My mom smiled, pulling me in a hug "it's fine, Zhera." I nuzzled my head in her arms whispering "thank you."

—

"My moms and I are finally talking, again"

"Yeah?" Aiden hummed, reaching out to fix a strand of hair that had fallen on my face.

"mhm, we talked and we're finally good. Is your dad still MIA?" I asked, absentmindedly twisting my pencil on my finger.

We're currently in the school library, studying for the final exam.

Aiden scratched his head, his expression filled with a mix of uncertainty . "A bit, but it's not the same as before. I'll just give it some time."

I could tell Aiden wanted to mend his relationship with his dad, especially after he told him about not wanting to pursue professional football.

"He'll eventually come around," I reassured him, my attention shifting back to my work.

"Wrong, Thompson." Aiden said pointing at my paper, where I was writing the definition of the molecular mechanisms underlying the regulation of cell cycle progression in eukaryotic cells.

"Is it not this?"

As he leaned closer to me, I couldn't help but notice the alluring scent of his cologne, that irresistible vanilla aroma that seemed to envelop the space around us.

It was a scent that had become glued with him, always present and comforting.

I couldn't help but notice that a few buttons on his uniform were undone, revealing a glimpse of his toned chest. The sleeves of his shirt were rolled down, emphasizing the definition of his arms as they flexed with each movement he made. The veins on his arms were subtly visible.

How did he manage to look so effortlessly hot? All he was doing was helping me but he still managed to look so attractive.

As I was captivated by Aiden, I found myself lost in the moment, unable to hear the words that escaped his lips. It was as if time stood still.

How did i even manage to bag a guy like this? God i'm so lucky

Suddenly, I was snapped out of my daze by the feeling of his lips pressing against mine. Confusion washed over me as I turned towards Aiden, searching for an explanation. With a hint of amusement in his eyes, he pulled away "You weren't listening to me."

I tried to process what had just happened. Aiden, noticing my confusion, gently placed his hand on my cheek and leaned in closer, his lips brushing against mine once more. "I'm sorry," he whispered, "I just wanted to make sure you were paying attention."

I awkwardly smiled, feeling a flutter of butterflies in my stomach. "S-sorry, can you repeat that?"

"The answer is option A," he began. "It involves a complex network of molecular mechanisms that coordinate the activities of CDKs, cyclins, and checkpoint proteins."

Fuck i'm doomed, I was always good at science but these days with everything going on my mind has been somewhere else.

Feeling overwhelmed, I took a long sip of my coffee, hoping it would somehow provide me with the mental clarity I desperately needed.

A groan escaped my lips as I realized the caffeine boost wasn't doing much to help my confusion.

"You're drinking way too much coffee, Thompson," Aiden chuckled, pulling me closer by the waist. "It's not going to help. don't worry, I'll help you, okay?"

"okay." I whispered sitting up straight. I don't know how Aiden does it. After all that's going on with his dad and sports he still manages to stay focus and help me.

—

We continued studying for a couple more hours,and I was finally getting to understand it more. As the time to leave finally arrived, Aiden insisted on walking me back home.

"Alright, bye," I said tiredly, waving at him before turning to head inside.

But just as I was about to step through my front door, Aiden reached out and grabbed my hand, causing me to pause.

"Wait," he said, "I have to tell you something."

"Yeah? What is it?"

Aiden took a deep breath, his eyes locked with mine. "My mom wants to meet you," he revealed, a smile tugging at the corners of his lips. "She's inviting you to dinner tomorrow."

—

Wordcount: 1276

42 | Mrs.Miller

After Aiden shared the news with me, my tiredness seemed to vanish, replaced by a surge of worry that kept me up all evening. Thoughts of meeting his mom as his girlfriend now rather than just a "friend" swirled through my mind. I was nervous but at the same time exited.

Aiden's advice to not think too much about it was impossible to follow. How could I not think over what to wear and how to prepare? Feeling overwhelmed, I remembered I have two amazing best friends to help.

"I have no idea what to wear, guys," I groaned, staring at the array of clothes in my closet, even though I have a decent amount of clothes, it seemed like I had no options or that they all fell short for this special occasion. The struggle to find the perfect outfit was real.

"Wear something formal but cute." Ciara said, being the fashion experts she is

Kehlani reassured me, "just don't stress. I heard Mrs. Miller is a very nice person."

"Yeah, she's nice," I replied, feeling a weight lifted off my shoulders. I didn't have to worry so much, but I still wanted to make a good first impression as his girlfriend.

"I should properly bring something, like a gift right?"

"definitely, I heard parents love that."

I started pulling out different outfits, trying them on and assessing how they made me feel. Each one seemed to have its drawbacks - too casual, too formal, not flattering enough, or simply not feeling right for the occasion.

It was a battle between wanting to look effortlessly put together and not wanting to seem like I was trying too hard.

After what felt like an eternity of trying on different clothes, I finally found an outfit that was just right. It was stylish and cute, without being too over-the-top. When I looked at myself in the mirror, I felt confident and comfortable.

I settled on a cozy, button-up blue sweater that hugged my curves just right. It had a touch of elegance, perfect for the occasion. Paired with a black skirt. Since it was winter, I decided to wear black tights underneath to keep warm without sacrificing style.

"Alright, guys, I'm all set! Ciara, I took your advice and decided to keep the black tights."

Ciara let out an excited squeal, "Thank you! I knew I was right."

"Time is ticking, it's almost 6," Khelani urged urgently.

Before ending the call, I sent them a virtual kiss and thanked them for their help.

—

I nervously ringed the doorbell, holding the wine carefully on my arms. As I stood awkwardly at the door, I couldn't help but be in awe of the house. It was adorned with beautiful holiday decorations, creating a magical atmosphere.

Just a few moments later, Mrs. Miller opened the door, and my eyes were immediately drawn to her stunning off-the-shoulder knit sweater, perfectly paired with comfy jeans.

"Hi honey!" she exclaimed, enveloping me in a warm hug. Returning the embrace, I greeted her with a smile, "Hello, Mrs. Miller. How are you?"

She gently corrected me, "I told you to call me Madelyn, but I'm doing alright." Then, she took my hand and invited me inside.

The inside looked even better. It was also decorated like the outside but looked even cozier. I noticed the soft glow of candlelight and the inviting aroma of a home-cooked meal

"I thought you might enjoy some wine,"I offered, presenting the bottle with a smile.

Her eyes widened with surprise as she exclaimed, "I love it! Thank you, honey." She then delicately placed the bottle down. "I know you're wondering where Aiden is, he was taking a bath, but i'm sure he's done by now, you can go call him down."

I noded and made my way upstairs to his room. Almost getting lost up from the millions of rooms up here.

Finally reaching his door, I raised my hand to knock, but then hesitated. The light spilling from beneath the door showed that he was done with his bath.

"Aiden, you there?" I called out, my voice echoing through the hallway. As I pushed the door open, my words trailed off and my steps faltered. There he stood, shirtless.

I couldn't help but let my eyes wander a bit. His perfectly sculpted abs were on full display, glistening under the soft glow of the room's light. Every muscle seemed to be perfectly defined, It was hard not to appreciate the sight before me.

The air seemed to still as our eyes met, and for a moment, time itself held its breath. My mind raced to find the right words, but all that escaped my lips was a soft exhale of surprise.

"Earth to Thompson." He snapped me out of my thoughts. The atmosphere in the room shifted as soon as his voice broke through my daydreaming.

" Put a shirt on." I grumbled while looking away.

"I was about too, but someone came in my room." He then smirked "and you don't have to look away, sweetheart."

I stayed glued to the door, my heart racing. The silence was deafening, and I couldn't help but feel like someone was lurking just out of sight.

"well, your mom said to tell you to come down, okay bye." I turned around to leave, but Aiden stopped me.

"come here."

Fiddling with my hands, unsure of what to say or do. Aiden had a way of making me feel like I was on the edge of a cliff, and I was always afraid of falling off. But there was something about him that made me feel safe, too. I made my way closer to him, my heart pounding in my chest.

"what is it?"

"come closer." He reached his hand out and I instinctively intercepted it. He drew me closer by the waist, then leaned down, his lips tracing delicate kisses from my collarbone to my neck, up to my jaw, and finally my cheek. I was feeling butterflies as he drew closer, and our lips finally met. A rush of emotions enveloping me

The kiss began gently but soon turned passionate. His hands held my waist firmly, prompting a gentle response from me as I explored his body with my hands, eventually moving them around his neck. When I lightly grasped a part of his neck, he let out a soft moan, deepening our kiss and embrace.

I felt a surge of excitement as his hands moved down to my leg, almost causing me to lose my balance. However, he quickly steadied me with a touch that was both firm and gentle. Aiden then softly bit my lips before trailing kisses down to my neck, leaving tender marks.

As I felt Aiden's warm breath on my neck, I struggled to find the words to remind him of his mom waiting downstairs. "Aiden," I managed to say breathlessly, my voice barely above a whisper.

He looked up at me, still nibbling on my neck, and murmured a soft "hm?"

"We have to go downstairs, your mom's waiting,"I reminded him. Aiden pulled back with a groan, clearly out of breath. "Ahh, I forgot."

He then tried to adjust his breathing. His chest rose and fell with each labored breath. "Go ahead, I have to take care of something." Before I left, I planted one last lingering kiss on his lips and reluctantly left the room.

I couldn't help but smile, my mind filled with the memory of his lips on mine. It was a type of kiss we hadn't shared since the beginning of our relationship. However, my smile faded as I noticed the marks he left on my neck. Fuck, I hope they're not too visible. Before descending the stairs, I hastily adjusted my sweater and wiped my lips.

"He's coming soon, Madelyn."

—

Wordcount: 1317

43 | Aiden's interior

The dinner started off a bit awkward between Aiden and I after, you know, what happened in his room.

Mrs. Miller, bless her heart, was doing most of the talking, trying to break the ice.

"So, Zhera, has my son been treating you right?"

Aiden, who had barely said a word all evening, finally muttered, "Of course, I have, Mom." Mrs. Miller clarified that she wasn't asking him directly.

I took a breath and replied, "Yes, he does."

Aiden smiled while looking at his mom. "that's good to know, he better be." She said eyeing him, then turned towards me

"Well, i've been willing to know how this son of mine asked you to be his girlfriend?"

Aiden paused mid-bite, his expression showing a hint of embarrassment. I could sense that he wasn't satisfied with how it happened. But honestly,

I didn't need anything extravagant or over-the-top. We were hanging out together, enjoying each other's company, when it happened.

"We were just hanging out and it happened."

Aiden's mom couldn't hide her surprise as she tapped him on the head, "Is this how I raised you?" Aiden, slightly flustered, scratched his head and attempted to explain himself, "Mom, I was going to-"

But before he could finish his sentence, his mom interrupted, "I've heard enough of you." She then turned her attention towards me "Don't worry, he'll come up with something better."

I couldn't help but chuckle as I took a bite of my steak, trying to ease the tension. "It's fine, really."

But his mom wasn't convinced. She shook her head and firmly stated, "No, it isn't fine. No child of mine will ask a girl out like that, nope, especially not his first girlfriend."

The realization hit me like a wave, catching me off guard. I couldn't help but feel a twinge of surprise, I'm Aiden's first?, though, it made sense. Aiden had never talked about having a girlfriend before, and he seemed to avoid interactions with girls. Could it be that he had been intentionally keeping his distance, for me? The thought filled me with warmth.

Glancing at Aiden, who was now looking a bit sheepish, and I could tell he was thinking of how to make it right. Even though there was nothing to make right. I liked it

—

The rest of the dinner went well. Madelyn couldn't stop talking and sharing embarrassing stories about Aiden. One of them in particular was when Aiden realized that he had a crush on me so he kept on talking about me every chance he got, he thought he was slick and that no one knew but everyone did. Except for me

When it was time to clean up, I offered to help, even though Madelyn kept telling me it was fine. I insisted anyway. Aiden was in the kitchen, doing the dishes.

But here's the thing, Aiden seemed off. He was unusually quiet throughout dinner, not making any cheeky remarks and barely smiling. Something's definitely up. I just don't know how to bring it up

Madelyn reached out and touched my hand, trying to comfort me. "Don't stress too much about him," she said, her voice filled with concern. "Honestly, it stresses me out too."

"What do you mean?"

Letting out a tired sigh, Madelyn explained, "He's always been the type to keep things to himself. He hardly tells anyone anything, not even me, his own mother." She chuckled and shook her head. "He definitely gets that from his father."

I nodded as I continued cleaning the table, lost in my thoughts. Madelyn's words made me realize how much Aiden was going through.

"To be honest, he's still stuck on what happened to his brother, they were really close, you know, but when I ask him if he wants to talk about it, he tells me there's more important things that I should be worried about. God, that boy."

So that's how Aiden has been feeling all these months? I knew he was still impacted by his brothers death, I just didn't know how to make him feel better.

The fact that he's an outgoing and loud person on the outside, while being very private on the inside, shows how much he's keeping things bottled up inside.

After we finished tidying up, I excused myself and made my way to the kitchen.

"Aiden."

"Are you staying? Zhera" He asked making his way towards me

"Should I?

"I want you to," he replied, his voice carrying a certain tone that caught my attention. The look in his eyes also showed that something was different about him., I agreed, but not before asking my mom. Surprisingly, she said yes.

Maybe it was because Im eighteen now and because she trusts Aiden. If it were any other time, or any other person my mom would have been furious and grounded me for even suggesting staying the night at a guy's place.

"She said yes." I exclaimed while entering his room, making sure to lock the door on my way in

Aiden was laying down on his bed, with one hand on his head, legs slightly apart. His eyes were closed, as if he was lost in thought.

The soft moon light from the nearby window illuminated his face, casting a gentle glow on his features. Aiden's hair was a messy cascade of dark strands, as he laid on the bed.

How could he look so hot, while just existing?

With a subtle nod and a smile, Aiden's gaze met mine. In that moment, he reached out his hand, and without hesitation, I took it. He then sat up straight.

"I'm happy you're staying the night." Aiden said while wrapping his arms around my waist, pulling me into a tight embrace. With a gentle smile on my face, I reached up and ruffled his hair.

The room seemed to be filled with an air of comfort, as if we had found solace in each other's presence. The soft touch of his arms around me and the way he held me close made me feel safe.

In that moment, all worries and stresses melted away, replaced by a sense of comfort. It was like time had paused just for us, allowing us to enjoy the simple time of being together.

"Aiden," I called out, capturing his attention. He responded with a simple, "Hm?" I gently guided him away from the embrace and sat down beside him.

"Are you okay?"

Confusion flickered in his eyes, "What do you mean?" I took a moment to gather my thoughts. "You haven't been yourself today," I explained hoping he would open up

Aiden let out a light chuckle. "Was it that obvious?" he asked. I nodded.

He let out a sigh and leaned back. "Things have been overwhelming lately, especially with my dad."

I listened carefully, giving him the space to share more.

"He's still not talking to me," he continued, his voice heavy with disappointment and a bit of sadness. "Things have been very bad between us." His hand instinctively reached up to rub his temples.

"And don't get me started on college," he added, frustration lacing his tone. "The ones I applied for didn't reply back, and it's been a while now, if I don't get into at least three of those, i'm never going to hear the end of it, with my dad."

"I sometimes feel like maybe I made the wrong mistakes not pursuing professional football."

I layed down beside him, staring straight at the ceiling. "you always act like everything is fine, especially when it's not."

"that's just how i am."

A heavy sigh escaped my lips as I shifted, resting my head on his chest, feeling the steady rhythm of his heartbeat. "It makes me feel guilty," I confessed. "You're always there for me, listening to my problems, but I never know what's going on with you. It makes me feel a bit helpless."

He gently stroked my hair, his touch bringing comfort. "That's because I don't open up to anyone," he admitted softly.

"Promise me that you'll share your problems with me, like you did today," I pleaded, a slight frown on my face.

Aiden chuckled warmly, his laugh soothing my worries. "Alright, pinky promise," he agreed, intertwining his pinky finger with mine. Then, with a small gesture, he leaned down and planted a kiss on my forehead.

—

Wordcount: 1400

44 | Holidays

As the night went on, we talked about different things and stuff that weighed on Aiden's mind. I gave him reassurance about his dad and his worries about college, assuring him that everything would work out in the end.

It was then that I saw a side of Aiden that he had never shown anybody else—a side that was private and vulnerable that he had never even shown with his mother or his closest friends.

He told me that he wanted to study engineering, and he applied to Princeton, Harvard, and Yale. He specifically wanted to be a neuroengineer or a biomedical engineer, which is something I never thought he would be interested in.

It felt like our relationship deepened, and with each passing moment, my affection for him grew stronger. It was as if our bond had transformed to a new level, and I found myself falling even more deeply in love.

—

"You spent what at his house?" Khelani gasped, her eyes going wide with shock.

I laughed tensely as a blush started to appear on my cheeks. "The night," I answered back.

With her eyebrows raised, Ciara exited the changing room. She chastised me, asking, "And it's now that you tell us?" I approached her and smiled shyly as I adjusted her dress. "It happened like two days ago; I just didn't get the chance to say it."

Khelani leaned closer, her interest peaked, and her smile got bigger. "Did you guys..." she began, hinting at something in her tone.

My face flushed even more, and I shook my head to cut her off. "No way!" I cried out, trying not to look embarrassed. It hasn't even been a month since we started dating; how could she think that?

I doubt Aiden was contemplating sex at all, and I wasn't even thinking about it. Whatever, it was way too early for that.

Ciara laughed out loud and nudged me. "Our Zhera here was thinking something else, huh?" she quipped.

"Guys," I murmured while attempting to hide my embarrassment.

They both laughed and apologized, realizing they had taken the conversation in a whole other direction. We continued shopping, their laughter echoing through the store.

As we strolled through the stores, I realized that Christmas was just around the corner. I still hadn't found the perfect gifts for my parents and friends, but I decided to worry about Khelani and Ciara's presents another day. My main focus was finding something special for Aiden, but I was completely clueless about what to get him.

Once Ciara found the dress she needed for the Christmas party her parents had planned, or the banquet, as she liked to call it, which was later tonight, we continued strolling around. As we walked, I couldn't help but voice my concern to them.

"I'm completely stuck, guys. I have no clue what to get him."

Ciara chimed in, suggesting, "Just get him something expensive, like a watch."

I hesitated, realizing that Aiden wasn't really into lavish or pricey things. I noticed that he appreciated more thoughtful gestures, like giving something related to his interests.

I pondered about Aiden's daily activities. He plays football, but it wasn't practical to give him another football since he probably had plenty. He wears glasses, but that doesn't seem right either. Ah! I remembered seeing him with a book in hand, and his room had a massive bookshelf.

And then it hit me—a bookmark! It seemed like the perfect idea, don't you think? He likes books, so I got him a bookmark.

"Guys, what about a bookmark?"

They stopped in their tracks, seemingly surprised. "Wait, you're serious? A bookmark?" Ciara questioned.

"Yes, I am."

Kehlani interrupted, understanding the situation. "Hold on, he's your boyfriend, right? If you believe a bookmark is something he'll appreciate, then go for it, Z."

Ciara looked at the both of us and simply smiled, shaking her head. I know that look; she did not agree with my choice, but I don't care; I think he'll like it. Even though I was always told that I was horrible at gifting good gifts to people, I'm confident about this one.

"Anyways, guys, can we hit up this store? My mom told me to give gifts to each of my teachers, including Mr.Robert." Khelani said, stopping in front of a store.

"Not, mister Robert, Kehlani don't." Ciara said it with a look of disgust.

If you're curious, Mr.Robert is that weird teacher that every school has; he looks at the girls weirdly and makes backhanded comments, even though he has a whole wife and kids. Weird and disgusting, I know.

"Don't worry, I won't; he doesn't deserve shit."

"You should gift him shit."

—

"So, Ciara, how many people are going to be at this party?" Khelani asked while unloading her shopping bags.

Ciara was taken aback when she mentioned the word "party" and interrupted her with a stoic look.

"banquet"

"Yeah, banquet. How many people are going to be there?" Khelani asked

When she casually mentioned around sixty people, I couldn't help but snap my head towards her in surprise. "Sixty? Really, how many people do your parents know?"

Ciara giggled at my reaction and turned towards me. "A lot. Anyway, you know the Millers are coming?" she said, reminding me of Aiden's presence. It almost slipped my mind that Aiden, whose parents are business partners with Ciara's dad, would be coming too.

"Yeah, he told me," I replied with a smile, feeling excited about spending more time with Aiden. But it would also be the first time I would meet his dad.

Ciara chimed in with a mischievous smirk, "If you guys need some alone time, you can go to the third door on the second floor; no one goes there."

I groaned, "Ciara, please, we're going to be here with everyone else; there's no need for that."

"Yeah, sure," Khelani said while emerging from the closet, revealing her stunning red velvet dress. The fabric looked so soft and luxurious, and the sweetheart neckline accentuated her figure perfectly. The flared skirt added a playful touch, and the length falling just above her knees gave it a flirty vibe.

I couldn't help but exclaim, "Ahh, you look so cute!" as I made my way towards her. Ciara clapped her hands with a huge smile, mentioning that Alejandro would love it.

Khelani blushed. "I hope he does."

Oh yeah, speaking of Khelani and Alejandro, they were now dating, or at least it seemed that way. It was likely that he would ask her out today. I'm so happy my ship sailed.

"Hey girls, the guests are arriving; hurry up." Ciara's mom yelled from down the hall. We all started getting ready faster and made our way out of the room, but not before I admired my dress in the mirror. It was a simple white dress with a pretty fitted silhouette that hugged all the right curves.

The fabric was soft and had a slight sheen to it, adding an extra touch of allure. The dress had an off-the shoulder neckline, and the back had a low cut with crisscrossing straps. The length was just below my knee. It was the perfect combination of sexy and cute. I felt very confident in it.

I stopped in my tracks when I spotted Aiden entering the door. A smile spread on my face.

—

only about two chapters left, then the story is done. Stop i'm going to cry ;(

Wordcount: 1251

45 | Whispers of trust

He's wearing a sleek black tuxedo that fits him perfectly, accentuating his tall frame. The crisp white shirt peeks out from under the jacket. His hair is styled nicely, it looked like he was going for a more wet look.

I then noticed a girl make her way towards him with her phone out and that was my cue to go greet him.

As I approached him, I could feel the air crackling. He was like a magnet, drawing my gaze and capturing my heart in an instant. Amidst the crowd, he noticed me making my way towards him, and everything else seemed to fade into the background. His focus was solely on me, his eyes locking with mine, as if we were the only two people in the room.

"Hi sweetheart." Those words, spoken with such tenderness, sent shivers down my spine. And then, in a moment that felt suspended in time, he leaned in and planted a gentle kiss on my cheek.

The girl, who had been trying for his attention, let out a frustrated groan, but he paid her no attention. His unwavering focus on me made me feel like the most important person in his universe.

I couldn't help but notice how good he looked, and as I took a closer look at his outfit, it only enhanced his charm. "You look good, today."

"same to you." He replied looking me up and down with a smile.

Just as we were lost in our own little world, a tall man entered the room, and I could feel Aiden tense up beside me. This man had an air of distinction about him, a charisma that was impossible to ignore. His salt-and-pepper hair added a touch of wisdom to his appearance, and the lines on his face showed his older age.

The way he carried himself, with confidence and grace, caught everyone's attention. Every step he took commanded respect. His eyes, a deep shade of gray, held an intense gaze that seemed to penetrate through you.

Aiden let out a sigh, "Ah, that's my dad." It was clear that they shared a resemblance, even though their features were a bit different. Aiden took after his mom more in terms of looks. You could still tell he was his dad.

As he approached, I couldn't help but feel a tinge of nervousness. This was the moment to greet him, to make a good impression. "Good afternoon, sir," I greeted him, my voice laced with a hint of awkwardness.

He looked down at me for a brief moment, his gaze piercing yet curious. Then, he nodded and spoke, "Good afternoon, Zhera, right?"

My eyes widened in surprise. He knew my name? How did he know? But I quickly composed myself and managed a light smile.

"Yes, it's nice to meet you," I replied, trying to mask my astonishment.

I couldn't help but wonder how he knew my name. Maybe Aiden had mentioned me in their conversations, or maybe he had seen us together before.

"Nice to meet you too, I hope everything is going well with my son?"

I mustered a smile, "Yes, things are amazing." I glanced up at Aiden, who seemed to be trying his best to remain calm, though the tension between him and his dad was palpable.

His dad nodded at my response, wishing me a good afternoon before continuing further into the room. Aiden let out a sigh, as if he had been holding everything in. It was clear that there was still some unresolved tension between them, and I hope that one day they would be able to fix things.

"well that was awkward." I muttered under my breath, then glanced up a Aiden "everything okay?"

He smiled "yeah, let's go in."

"you go ahead, I have to stay here and greet the rest of the guest, okay?"

Aiden noded and made his way further into the house were the banquet took place, not before he gave me a peck.

—

"Oh my gosh, are those the twins?" I exclaimed, my eyes widening as I caught sight of Mason and Liam Alderidges entering the room. They were both dressed in matching tuxedos.

Curiosity got the better of me, and I turned to Ciara, "Do your parents know them?" I couldn't help but be curious by the connection between the Alderidges and her family.

Ciara let out a groan, clearly exasperated. "Yup, our families know each other. I've known them since childhood," she explained, her tone filled with a mix of annoyance and familiarity.

Kehlani and I exchanged a glance, both of us surprised by this. "Now you tell us?" we exclaimed.

If you didn't already know, the twins are from a very wealthy family called the Alderidges. They're known to be secretive and have a long history, with rumors even saying that they may be descendants of royalty. Having any connection with them is considered very lucky.

She shrugged "it just didn't seem like an important thing to mention."

Just as we were processing the news about the Alderidges, We found ourselves face-to-face with Ciara's dad. Kehlani quickly fixed her hair and flashed a smile.

"Hi Mr. Daniel," we both chimed in unison.

He returned our greeting with a hello before turning his attention to Ciara. "Honey, I want you to go greet the Alderidges twins, it's been a while since you've seen them."

"wish me luck, guys." Ciara groaned then made her way towards them. As Ciara approached, the twins spotted her and eagerly made their way towards her. I think it was Mason who excitedly took hold of her hand, causing her to blush.

Kehlani and I exchanged a knowing look, sensing that there was definitely something going on between them.

With Ciara off to greet the twins, Kehlani took the opportunity to engage with Mr. Daniel. She flashed him a smile and asked if there was anything we could help him with.

"No it's alright, you two can go do your own things now." He then walked away

"What a man." I heard Kehlani whisper under her breath. I turned towards her with a perplexed look. She giggled and quickly dismissed it, saying, "You didn't hear that." Then, she spotted Alejandro and made her way towards him, bidding me farewell.

Now I was left alone, as I looked around, I couldn't spot Aiden anywhere. I checked the table where he was supposed to be, but it was only his parents there. I knew Aiden well enough to realize that he's not a fan of big gatherings like this. So, I figured he must have slipped away to find some peace outside.

I didn't waste a second and made my way through the crowd, grabbing my jacket on the way. Stepping outside, I scanned the area, hoping to catch a glimpse of Aiden.

And there he was, sitting on the patio chairs, head tilted back, lost in the vastness of the sky. It was like he found his own little sanctuary away from the chaos of the event.

"Hey Aiden," I greeted him, settling down next to him on the patio chairs. He responded with a simple "Hi Zhera," his gaze still fixated on the mysterious night sky. As if seeking comfort, he leaned his head against my shoulder, creating a sense of closeness between us.

"you should've brought a jacket, it's freezing."

"I feel warmer now, with you."

In the moment, time seemed to stand still as we sat there together, finding comfort in each other's company. The darkness of the night enveloped us, allowing us to escape the noise and distractions of the party. The gentle breeze danced through the air, carrying whispers of calmness.

As we sat side by side, a comfortable silence settled between us. Words were unnecessary; just silence that spoke words. It was as if we had created our own little universe, where worries and troubles didn't exist exist. We reveled in the simple pleasure of being present, sharing this moment in each other's presence.

The stars above us shimmered, like tiny fragments of hope scattered across the vast night. It made me feel safe.

Minutes turned into hours, yet it felt like only seconds had passed. We were lost in our own world, cherishing the quietness and understanding we found in each other. The weight of our worries and stress seemed to lift, replaced by a sense of reassurance.

In this moment, I couldn't help but feel grateful for the bond we shared. As the night continued to unfold. So did our thoughts and feelings

"I like this, being here with you." He said, breaking the silence, while playing with my fingers

"I feel the same way," I responded, a smile spreading across my face. The warmth of his touch as he played with my fingers sent a comforting tingle through my body. We both knew that this moment, away from the chaos of the party, was something special.

As if sensing the depth of our emotions, Aiden lifted his head from my shoulder, his eyes meeting mine. In that instant, time seemed to slow down. The soft touch of his lips against mine sent a wave of warmth and tenderness coursing through my veins.

The kiss lingered for a moment, a sweet and gentle connection that spoke volumes without the need for words. As his hands gently caressed my cheeks, his touch sent shivers down my spine, and I couldn't help but smile. My heart raced, knowing that this kiss was different from the others. Maybe it was the cold air that made it feel more special, or it was the fact that we weren't in the best mood earlier. Whatever it was, this kiss brought a sense of comfort and reassurance.

After we finally pulled away, our eyes locked in a gaze. I could see the sincerity in his eyes, and my heart skipped a beat as he spoke those words, "I want to take you somewhere, tomorrow, can I?"

The excitement bubbled within me, and I exhaled a breath I didn't realize I was holding. "Yeah," I replied. I couldn't help but wonder where he had in mind.

As I looked into his eyes, I could sense his genuine enthusiasm and the effort he had put into planning whatever he was thinking off. The thought of spending more time together, made me happier.

With a soft smile, I leaned in closer, our foreheads touching as I whispered, "I can't wait." Then gave him another kiss.

"Oh, I almost forgot something!"I reached into my bag, a smile playing on my lips, as I pulled out the little surprise I had prepared for Aiden. holding up the handmade bookmark I had crafted just for him. "here! happy Christmas!"

Aiden's eyes widened with curiosity as he looked at the gift in my hands. "A bookmark?" he asked, a hint of surprise in his voice.

I nodded eagerly. "Yep! I noticed how much you love reading, and I also noticed that you never seem to have a bookmark handy when you need one. So, I decided to take matters into my own hands and make you one"

Aiden's smile grew soft as he took a closer look at the bookmark.

"I know it's not the best but-" Before I could even finish my sentence, Aiden wrapped his arms around me in a tight embrace

"You know," he began, "it may just be a simple bookmark, but it means so much more to me because you made it. Anything you do is amazing to me, sweetheart."

—

guys two more chapter and we're done…so i'm trying to make the last ones longer

Wordcount: 1952

46 | Deja vû

The next day

He let out a cough, his voice strained with regret. "Thompson, I'm sorry," Aiden said, his words interrupted by a sniffle.

"I told you, you should've brought your jacket," I responded, a hint of frustration in my voice. "I know, I know, I'm sorry; please forgive me," he pleaded.

"If you weren't such a dumbass and didn't decide to go into the freezing cold without a jacket, this wouldn't have happened." I could hear him sniffle on the other end of the line. We were in the midst of talking about our plans for the day, which had been disrupted by Aiden's dumbass decision to not wear a jacket tomorrow, which made him sick.

"Are you going to be alone?" I asked

"My parents aren't here, yeah."

"Okay, I'll be there," I assured him. Without giving him a chance to ask any questions, I ended the call.

—

As I approached the front door, I raised my hand to knock, but before I could make contact, the door swung open widely, revealing a devastated Aiden. His usually nice hair was dishevelled, as if he had been running his fingers through it for hours. His eyes, usually bright, were now a bit red. His whole body seemed to slump, as if the weight of the world was resting on his shoulders.

As I entered the house, a chuckle escaped my lips at the sight of Aiden's dishevelled appearance. "Is that how you look when you're sick?" I couldn't help but tease, taking in the scene around me.

Aiden's voice, tinged with exhaustion and irritation, snapped me back to reality. "Don't make fun of me, Thompson," he replied.

Quickly realizing my mistake, I reassured him, "No, no, I didn't mean it that way. I'm sorry, Aiden." Placing my bags on the kitchen counter, I began taking out the ingredients.

Curiosity got the better of him, and he peered over my shoulder, asking, "What are you doing?"

I shifted slightly, not wanting him to invade my personal space. "I'm making food. You mentioned that you haven't eaten all day, right? Let me make something up for you." I pulled out an apron, ready to get started.

Aiden's surprise was evident in his voice as he exclaimed, "Why am I only finding out now that you can cook, sweetheart?"

With a shrug, I replied, "I only know the basics, but I'll give it my best shot. Cooking can be fun, you know."

And so, with an apron on and determination in my eyes, I set out to prepare a meal for him. The kitchen became a hub of activity as I chopped, stirred, and seasoned, hoping to create something delicious for Aiden's body.

20 minutes later

"What on earth is that?" he asked, his eyes fixed on the "food" sizzling away on the stove. I let out a sigh and shook my head in disappointment.

"Honestly, I have no clue," I replied, my voice tinged with a mix of confusion.

The sight on the stove was a total bummer. We were faced with a mishmash of random ingredients, all thrown together without any rhyme or reason. There were these blobs of tofu swimming in a green sauce and a tangled mess of overcooked spaghetti noodles that clung together like they were glued. And to add insult to injury, there were these burnt onions scattered all over, giving off a nasty, charred smell.

Aiden's laughter filled the room, and I couldn't help but join in, my chuckles blending with his. But as his laughter continued, a frown crept onto my face.

"If you keep laughing like that, that hyena laugh or yours, I swear I'm out of here," I grumbled, crossing my arms defiantly.

His laughter gradually stopped, and then he surprised me by wrapping his arms around me from behind. "I'm sorry, sweetheart. Please don't leave," he pleaded, his voice filled with sadness, but I could tell he was trying to suppress a laugh.

I shifted slightly, not wanting to catch his cold, but the warmth of his embrace was too enticing to resist. We stood there, wrapped in each other's arms.

"Okay, that's enough," I remarked, pinching his hands as he started planting light kisses along my neck. "I'm not trying to get sick again," I added, dropping a hint about when I got sick not long ago.

Aiden looked at me with a grin and said, "It would be good if you did get sick again, so I can take care of you once more."

"No thanks; anyway, what do we do with this mess?" I groaned looking at the thing I just created; something must have gone wrong while I was cooking. Yes, I always knew my skills weren't the best, but I never knew it was this bad.

"Don't worry," Aiden whispered, his hands reaching for the utensils on the stove. "I'll make something."

"No, you're sick. I can't let a sick person cook," I protested, concern etching my face.

He gestured for me to sit on the chair, his touch gentle as he guided me onto it. "I'm feeling better now, thanks to your presence, and you've already done more than enough; just sit back and relax, okay?"

I reluctantly nodded, but honestly, I was more worried about myself than him. I mean, he's the one who's sick, and I couldn't help but think, What if he accidentally contaminates the food?

But I trusted him and plopped down in the chair. It was in times like these that I loved how caring he was, making me feel all warm and cozy even when things were not the best.

As Aiden stood in the kitchen, a relaxed air surrounded him. His sleeves were rolled up, revealing his forearms, and a smile played on his lips. The aroma of herbs and spices filled the air as he chopped vegetables on the cutting board, his movements precise and effortless.

With every sizzle and sputter, the ingredients danced in the pan, the smell contaminating the kitchen. Aiden moved with grace, effortlessly flipping the food with a flick of his wrist.

I couldn't help but admire the way he seemed completely at home in the kitchen. Of course, he knew how to cook like this.

"Why is it now that I find out that you can cook?"

Aiden chuckled and shrugged his shoulders nonchalantly. "I don't tell people this," he confessed. I rolled my eyes. What does he tell people, then?

He then approached me with a spoon in hand, filled with steaming soup. The aroma alone made my mouth water. "Try this," he said, his voice filled with anticipation.

I eagerly took a spoonful of the soup, savouring the flavours on my taste buds. It was a perfect blend of spices. The warmth of the soup enveloped me, satisfying me with every sip.

"Perfect!" I exclaimed, unable to contain my satisfaction. Aiden, with a glint in his eyes, couldn't resist the temptation and planted a quick peck on my lips before swiftly retreating back to the stove.

"Aiden!" I exclaimed. With a frown, was it his mission to make me sick today? He turned around, a sheepish grin spreading across his face. "Sorry, I couldn't resist," he confessed.

I sighed, a playful smile tugging at the corners of my lips. "Wow, Miller, you really know how to push my buttons," I replied. Then I grabbed a paper towel and wiped my lips, making sure to give him a look.

Aiden winced, his eyes widening as he stared at me. "wow, really."

"I don't want to get sick; I already told you this." Changing the subject, I looked at him. "Anyway, is there anything I can help with?" I asked, feeling a bit useless just sitting here while he's sick and doing the cooking.

"You can sit there and look pretty for your boyfriend."

"Aiden."

Quickly realizing his slip-up, Aiden apologized, his tone shifting to a serious one. "Sorry, miss. You can, um, grab the juice inside the fridge," he quickly corrected himself.

Taking his suggestion, I made my way to the fridge and retrieved the juice. "Alright, got it. Now what?"

"Put it in a cup."

Following his instructions, I poured the juice into a cup, ready to bring it over to him. "Okay, it's in the cup. What now?" I asked, waiting for his next direction.

Aiden gestured for me to come closer. "Come here,"

I hesitated for a moment, not sure of what he was planning. But curiosity got the better of me, and I cautiously approached him. He then surprised me by opening his mouth, silently asking me to give him the cup.

"You're serious?" I asked, a mix of disbelief in my voice.

Aiden nodded, a grin spreading across his face. "What did you think it was for?" he replied, his tone filled with lightheartedness. "Look, I'm sick, and the least you can do is help me stay hydrated, right?"

I couldn't argue with his logic, and with a chuckle, I brought the cup of juice to his waiting lips. As he took a sip, I couldn't help but feel useful right now.

—

Soon enough, the food was done. And we started eating—well, I did. Aiden was currently weeping on his chair. I put down my spoon and looked at him. "What's wrong?"

He winced, his hand clutching his stomach. "It hurts to eat," he admitted, his voice strained. "I need help."

I could tell he was struggling, but a part of me suspected that he was using this as an opportunity to get me to feed him. Normally, I would scold him and tell him to tough it out, but seeing him in 'genuine' discomfort, I knew I had to be there for him. Even though he was probably lying

Without hesitation, I got up from my seat and sat beside him, placing a hand on his back. I picked up his spoon. "Let me help,"

As I held the spoon, I carefully scooped up a spoonful of the warm soup, making sure it was just the right temperature for him. I brought the spoon to his lips, my gaze locked with his.

He opened his mouth, and I gently fed him the spoonful of soup. I watched as his face softened, the pain momentarily forgotten as the flavours of the soup danced on his taste buds.

We continued this ritual. As I fed him, I couldn't help but notice the vulnerability in his eyes. It was obvious that he wasn't feeling well, plus, with all he was stressing about, he was trying to put up a brave face around me. He always does that.

Between spoonfuls, we exchanged smiles and shared glances, a silent understanding passing between us. Despite the discomfort he was experiencing, there was a sense of closeness that enveloped us.

As we continued, I could see a sense of relief wash over Aiden's face. The pain seemed to calm down, replaced by a sense of gratitude and appreciation. We finished the soup together, with the last spoonful marking the end of this moment.

I gently set down the spoon, my hand coming to rest on top of Aiden's. "Feeling better?"

He nodded, a small smile playing on his lips. "Thanks for helping me," he whispered. "But you know what else could make me feel even better?" He suddenly asked, a glint in his eyes.

I rolled my eyes, knowing Aiden's tendency. "What now?" I asked, pretending to be exasperated.

He leaned in closer. "A kiss," he said, his hands gesturing to his lips. I tilted my head. "Aiden, you know I don't want to get sick."

He sighed, disappointment evident on his face as he looked away. I couldn't resist his puppy-dog eyes, and with a groan, I gave in. I placed my hands on his cheeks, turned his face towards me, and planted a quick kiss on his cheek.

Aiden's face lit up with a smile as he turned back to face me. "That's better."

I couldn't help but laugh. "You're lucky; I can't resist you."

"I know."

—

For the rest of the day, we stayed in each other's comfort zone. We spent the rest of the evening talking, sharing stories, and just being present with each other. It was in these simple moments that our bond grew stronger, deepening our relationship.

Aiden told me how he and his dad are talking bit by bit and shared more about his brother's death and how he's coming to terms with it. All I could do was listen to him as he confessed his feelings and just be there for him.

As the night came to an end, I looked at Aiden with a soft smile. "Thank you for tonight," I said, my voice filled with genuine gratitude. "Even though you're not feeling well, you still managed to make me smile."

Aiden returned my smile, his eyes filled with affection. "It's all worth it if I can see you happy," he replied, his voice filled with sincerity.

"I felt like I should be saying that."

He smiled and gave me a hug. "I love you."

I can't believe it. Who would have thought that I'd end up here, spending the evening with Aiden, wrapped in each other's hands? I can't believe how far we've come. From constantly trying to outdo each other to this moment, where we're so close and connected,.

Our relationship grew when we began to recognize each other's strengths and weaknesses, and we learned how to uplift and encourage one another. This new perspective allowed us to grow together and build a bond that would stand the test of time.

Tonight, as we sit together in the quiet serenity of his house, the moment feels like the perfect time. Just the two of us—no one else to worry about. Just me and Miller.

—

47 | From rivals to lovers

----

5 months later

"Zhera Thompson," the principal's voice boomed through the speakers, causing a mix of excitement and nervousness to bubble up inside me. Taking a deep breath, I steadied myself and made my way up the grand staircase towards the podium.

As I climbed the stairs, I could feel the anticipation in the air. The crowd was buzzing with energy; their eyes were fixed on me. The sound of applause filled the place, growing louder and louder with each step I took. Amidst the sea of faces, I could pick out my dad's proud smile, his voice ringing out above the rest, cheering me on.

Reaching the podium, I looked out at the sea of familiar faces. Friends, teachers, and students all gathered together to celebrate this moment of graduation. The stage lights cast a warm glow, making me feel exhilarated and a little overwhelmed.

I took a moment to compose myself, my hands gripping the edges of the podium for support. The cheers calmed down, and a hush fell over the room as all eyes were now fixed on me. It was a strange feeling, standing there as the centre of attention.

With a quick glance at my notes, I began to speak, my voice steady. I shared my gratitude for the support of my family, friends, and teachers who had guided me throughout my journey. I expressed my appreciation for the opportunities and challenges that had shaped me into the person I had become.

As I spoke, I could feel the energy in the room building again. Applause erupted, and cheers filled the air, encouraging me to continue. The words flowed effortlessly, as if the crowd's enthusiasm was helping my confidence.

I shared stories of wins and setbacks, highlighting the lessons I had learned along the way. The crowd hung onto my every word. It was a moment of reflection, a chance to celebrate not only my achievements but also the accomplishments of our entire school.

As I came to the end of my speech, I couldn't help but feel pride. The cheers grew even louder, echoing through the place, as the crowd showed their appreciation for my words.

Stepping away from the podium, I felt a mixture of relief. The weight of the moment lifted from my shoulders, replaced by a sense of peace. I made my way back down the stairs, greeted by hugs.

"That was incredible, Zhera!" my friends exclaimed, enveloping me in a tight hug. The overwhelming rush of emotions threatened to spill over, but I tried my best to hold back the tears. It was hard to believe that this was the end of our high school journey, and soon we would all be on different paths.

"Thanks, you guys," I managed to say, my voice trembling slightly. Khelani reached out to wipe away my tears, but her own tears started flowing uncontrollably.

"Aw, don't cry, Z," she sniffled. We were all feeling the weight of this bittersweet moment, the mixture of joy and sadness intertwining in our hearts.

Ciara couldn't help but make a sarcastic remark. "I can't believe I'm surrounded by a bunch of crying babies," she teased, though her own tears betrayed her.

Even in this moment of our lives, she maintained her cool, refusing to let her emotions show. "Oh, come on, Ciara," I chuckled through my tears. She was our rock, always keeping us grounded.

We let go, falling into silence. I can't believe it's done; this is the last time we're all going to be in the same school. Fuck, it does not feel real.

Just then. I spun around, recognizing that familiar voice. "Hi Thompson." There, he was making his way towards me with a huge bouquet of flowers on his hands.

"Hey, Miller," I replied with a grin, accepting the bouquet of flowers he offered. The vibrant colours and sweet fragrance instantly lifted my spirits.

"I liked your speech." I complimented Aiden's speech before mine; the school chose the both of us to give speeches since we were the best students, academically.

Aiden chuckled softly. "Well, to be honest, your speech wasn't half bad either," he teased.

"Oh, really, thank you, Miller; that means a lot." I sarcastically said this while playing with one of the flower petals. "The flowers are beautiful; thank you." He gave me a kiss on the forehead and said, "No problem."

I twirled the flowers on my hands. "I can't believe it's done."

"I know, it feels like a couple of months ago we were just talking about this moment; now it's finally here." He sighed while staring at the stage.

I nodded my head, glancing at the stage, then noticed Roman standing there, and right beside him was Myvy. And then, something unexpected happened. Roman moved his hands to her waist, pulling her closer and planting a gentle kiss on her cheek. They embraced each other in a hug, and my jaw dropped. All those suspicions I had about them were right. I felt a whirlwind of emotions, feeling a bit sad but also happy at the same time.

It's sad because our time together as a student council is over. We've had so many memories together, and I knew those two the longest out of everyone. But it's also a moment of happiness because my ship finally sailed.

I couldn't help but smile as I looked up at Aiden, feeling a sense of pride and accomplishment. But then, I noticed my parents making their way towards us, and my dad had tears in his eyes.

Aiden noticed it and chuckled. He gave me a kiss and made his way to where his parents were, waiting for him.

"We're so proud of you!" my mom exclaimed with a beaming smile. Seeing that look of pride on her face meant the world to me. It made me feel happy and proud that all the effort and hard work I had put in had finally paid off.

My dad chimed in, "You did it! All those late nights studying paid off!" We couldn't help but share tears of joy.

It's a memory that I will forever cherish, knowing that my parents were there by my side, celebrating this with me. My mom looked at me with teary eyes and said, "You know, seeing you up there on that stage, it feels like just yesterday when you were a little kid, taking your first steps. Time flies so fast." I squeezed her hand and said, "I know, Mom. It's hard to believe how much everything changes."

My dad joined the conversation, his voice filled with pride. "You've become such an incredible person, Zhera. We've watched you face challenges and grow into this amazing woman." I couldn't help but smile and say, "Thank you, guys." Their love and support mean everything to me, especially in this moment.

I glanced over at Aiden, who was in a conversation with his parents. It was a nice sight to see, knowing that he had finally mended his relationship with his dad after everything that happened months ago. His dad accepts and supports Aiden's decision to not pursue football professionally, and it was heartwarming.

I saw the look on Aiden's face when he told me that. He looked so happy.

Aiden's mom was overcome with emotion, and he was gently wiping away her tears. Meanwhile, his dad stood there with a smile, shaking his head. It was a beautiful moment, seeing them come together as a family and embrace the loss they had experienced.

Just as I was taking in the scene, I noticed Aiden and his dad making their way towards us. As they walked side by side, the resemblance between them was uncanny. Both stood tall and proud.

His dad greeted my parents, and then his gaze turned to me. "Congratulations, Zhera," he said. I replied awkwardly, "Thank you, sir." There was still a lingering sense of awkwardness between us, even though I've been dating his son for about half a year now.

"No problem; I just hope you two have a long-lasting relationship and wish you the best." With that, he left.

Leaving me in Star's truck, this was the first time he said something so nice to me and about our relationship. It felt nice getting the wishes of his dad.

—

We finally entered the dining hall after years of talking to people and thanking them for their congratulations.

The moment we stepped inside, we were greeted by elegant chandeliers, high ceilings, and beautiful decor. The walls are adorned with artwork, and the tables are set with fine china and fresh flowers. The ambiance is warm and inviting; it was really beautiful. There were only seniors here—everyone who graduated.

"Zhera, Aiden over there!" I heard Kehlani scream from where she was seated; beside her was Alejandro, and on her other side was Ciara, who was talking to one of the twins. She looked happy.

We made our way there and took our seats. Everything felt so overwhelming; this was the last time all of us would be here together. These that I've known for such long periods of my life, wow.

Juts then I felt a tap on my shoulders. Turning around, I was greeted with Myvy, who had a shy smile on her face. "Can I talk to you, Zhera?"

We then found a quiet spot. "I can't believe high school is over," I sighed.

Myvy's smile grew wider. "I know, it felt like it all went too fast, but I just wanted to tell you how much I've enjoyed having you as a classmate and student council member."

A warm feeling spread through me, and I couldn't help but smile back. "Thank you, Myvy. I'm going to miss high school and all the times we had. You know you were always my favourite."

Her giggle echoed in the air as she flashed that beautiful smile of hers. "You were mine too, Zhera."

We gave each other a tight squeeze before I noticed Roman in the distance, probably searching for her. "Hey, it looks like your guy is looking for you. You better go," I said, trying to hold back the emotions that were starting to well up inside me.

She let go and turned around, a big smile lighting up her face when she saw Roman. "Thanks! see you later," she replied. We shared one more quick hug before she hurried off to join him.

As I watched them hug, a wave of emotions washed over me. "Okay, Zhera, not the time for waterworks," I whispered to myself, trying to keep my composure.

Then I made my way back to the table; everyone was talking and just enjoying the last moments we had together. The dinner was going well.

—

As the night at the diner was winding down, Aiden squeezed my hands and gave me a grin. He whispered, "Wanna get out of this place?" I nodded eagerly. We excused ourselves, and I caught a knowing look from our friends Kehlani and Ciara.

Once we stepped outside, Aiden let out a sigh. "Feeling overwhelmed?" He nodded, and I reached out, inviting him to hold my hand. He smiled and intertwined his fingers with mine, and together, we started walking.

As we strolled hand in hand, enjoying the moonlight, Aiden pointed to the jewellery he gave me in New York. "Is that the one?" he asked, gently touching the piece in my hair. I nodded. I had matched the blue hair accessory with my baby blue dress.

Aiden grinned and leaned down to give me a sweet kiss. "You look beautiful," he whispered, filled with adoration.

I smiled back. As we continued our walk, hand in hand, we found ourselves
drawn to a familiar place. It was the library, the very spot where everything
started. Memories flooded my mind as I gazed at the grand entrance.

I couldn't help but chuckle as I recalled the moment when Aiden accidentally messed up my project in front of this very library. It was a
moment that brought us closer together. The library held a special place
in our relationship—a place where our paths crossed and our relationship
deepened.

We stood there in front of the library, taking in the quiet beauty of the
night. It was a moment of reflection and appreciation for how far we had
come.

I reached out and gently squeezed Aiden's hand. The library had witnessed
our growth, our laughter, and even our almost-kiss. It was a place filled
with memories, both big and small, that had shaped our relationship.

I turned to Aiden, my voice filled with a touch of sadness. "You know, out
of everything in this school, I think I'm going to miss this place the most."

Aiden nodded.It's always been my favourite spot too, especially when we
spent time here together."

I looked down, a smile tugging at the corners of my lips. "Yeah, it's amazing
how one assignment from Miss Marsha brought us together. I can't help
but wonder what would have happened if we hadn't been assigned to work
on that project."

Aiden shook his head gently, his grip on my hand tightening. "It's hard to
imagine, but I know one way or another we would've still ended uptogeth-
er."

As we stood there in front of the quiet library, surrounded by memories, I couldn't help but feel so grateful. It was like the universe had planned for us to grow closer through Miss Marsha's assignment. Our relationship grew right here in this place, and it's something I'll always treasure.

So, as we held hands, I knew that even though we were saying goodbye to everything, our bond would stay strong. The memories we made here will always have a special place in our hearts.

But who would have thought that I'd end up here, spending the evening with Aiden Miller, hand in hand? It's like a dream; it felt a bit surreal. I can't believe how far we've come. From constantly trying to outdo each other to this moment, where we're so close and connected,.

I used to see him as my biggest competitor, always trying to one-up each other. But now, it feels like none of that matters. We've discovered a deeper bond, something beyond academics.

It's funny how our rivalry brought us together in the first place. All those late nights studying and trying to outshine each other. But now, it feels like we've found something more meaningful.

This moment feels so right. All the tension and competition have faded away, leaving only warmth and affection. It's like we've rewritten our story, turning rivals into something so much more.

I'm grateful for our rivalry because it brought us here to this moment of vulnerability and tenderness. It's like we've discovered a whole new side of each other, one that goes beyond grades and achievements.

This evening, this moment feels like the perfect ending to our story. From rivals to friends, and now to something more. I'm ready to embrace this new chapter with open books.

The end